D1598999

THE
FOUNTAINS
OF NEPTUNE

BOOKS BY RIKKI DUCORNET

THE
FOUNTAINS
OF NEPTUNE

A novel by

RIKKI DUCORNET

Dalkey Archive Press

Originally published by McClelland & Stewart Inc., Canada

Library of Congress Cataloging-in-Publication Data
Ducornet, Rikki, 1943-
   The fountains of Neptune / Rikki Ducornet.
PS3554.U279F64   1992   813'.54—dc20   91-33554
ISBN: 0-916583-96-1

First American Edition, 1992

Partially funded by a grant from The Illinois Arts Council.

Dalkey Archive Press
1817 North 79th Avenue
Elmwood Park, IL 60635 USA

For my father, Gérard DeGré, Emperor
of d'Elir, and for Martin Provensen,
Keeper of Eden.

I wish to thank the Merrill Ingram Foundation and the Bunting Institute for their generous support. I also wish to thank Martha Cabral for taking me in when I had no place to go, Richard Martin for *das charybdische Sprudelbad*, and Ellen Seligman, Bernice Eisenstein, and Lee Davis Creal for their loving assistance.

Oliver Sacks' *Awakenings* came to my attention shortly after I conceived *The Fountains of Neptune*, and if I chose not to make the book a medical history – having perceived it from the start not as an historical novel but a work of the imagination – his beautiful book has informed my own.

"... For here, millions of mixed shades
and shadows, drowned dreams,
somnambulisms, reveries; all that we call
lives and souls, lie dreaming. ..."

– Herman Melville, *Moby Dick*

THE
FOUNTAINS
OF NEPTUNE

PART
I

It was Doctor Kaiserstiege who said that the world would perish because the accumulating traumas of human history were poisoning the human soul, just as morphine saturates the lungs and lunar caustic collects in deposits of metallic silver beneath the skin. It is true that Doctor Kaiserstiege's ideas were strange, but then nothing is stranger than reality; the reality of a life spent in dreaming. I am the one she called The Sandman, and I can only hope these hesitant pages, written by a phantom man, will shed new light on her bright volumes, those beautiful, moonstruck books some tried so hard to metamorphose into ashes.

My sleep began in the spring of 1914. I slept through both World Wars and the tainted calm between. It was as if I had been cursed by an evil fairy, pricked by an enchanted spinning wheel; an impenetrable briar had gripped my mind. The Doctor put it this way: she said I had taken a bite of the poison apple. She chose that apple deliberately. Knowledge – as much as its denial – had precipitated me headfirst into the land of Nod.

The Sandman, she wrote in *The Fountains of Neptune*, the volume devoted to my case, *lives in coma. In medicine, coma is defined as deep, unconscious sleep. In astronomy, it is that haze which veils the comet's nucleus. It is also the halo which wreathes an object as seen through an imperfect lens. In botany, coma is the silky beard at the end of certain seeds, even the whole head of a tree.*

I like all these definitions for the Sandman's coma. As any tree, he is a world unto himself; all that I do to rouse him (the bells, the cries, the clapping hands) only serves to animate his dreams. The waking world is that optical clarity he denies; he has veiled life's ice and fire in the preferable nebulosity of dreams.

One gazebo remains standing in the Doctor's south garden. I come here in warm weather to reflect. Once her gardens were allegories. Doctor Kaiserstiege believed that just as nature, the body of man can be brought to a state of harmony and tranquil health. LOVE AND SCIENCE can still be read above the infirmary door.

At the spa – her ideal universe – the elements themselves were domesticated: the sand neatly raked, the earth carpeted with grass, the air perfumed with roses; water tamed in basins, bathtubs, and wells. Even the sun's fire is still masked by gracious trees, arbours, and green glass. My gazebo has a latticed roof. And if I have not seen this place as it was intended to be seen, so it is for all men who gaze upon the world.

Water, both real and metaphorical, is in evidence everywhere. As the sun seeps from one empty hallway into another, one hundred cannellated columns reflected in as many mirrors, ripple. Even the ironwork of the garden fences, the kiosks and the gate, look like an abstraction of a water oily with eels. Her architects had created an aquatic maze of deep and shallow basins, secluded geysers spurting in violent spasms wherein one could crouch as naked as a god. This maze – destroyed in the Second War – is still talked about in the village because it fostered promiscuity.

As I attempt to weed K's overgrown garden paths, so do I put order to my memories, disentangling reality from dreams, and Heaven from Hell. These days I do nothing but attempt to interpret those enigmatic wheels, those churning shadows, those cries beyond cries; the story beneath all stories: my own.

Even now I hear shouting. I cannot say if it is my father's voice I hear or my mother's, or the voices of her assassins. A great clamour has been hammered into my soul and with every breath I hear it, even if – as the water's of K's crumbling fountains – it has been quieted; taught to murmur.

Nicolas, K wrote, *is the survivor of a triality and the witness to his family's tragedy. His answer is coma. One could not find a more poignant example of the Ego forsaking Itself.*

Late one summer's afternoon not long before Doctor Kaiser-stiege died, we were sitting together in the spa's vast pitted hall enjoying its mirrored coolness.

"We forget," she said, "that other mental states exist. We forget that thought is a process which has evolved over the ages from anterior states. Just as our finger-bones still resemble those of the lizard, so at depths deeper than dreaming our thoughts may echo the lobster's."

"Do lobsters dream?" I asked. "And barnacles?"

"Barnacles," K mused, "are female. To reproduce they grow the necessary appurtenance. Which seems frivolous for creatures who spend their lives stuck to the bottom of a boat."

"I am a barnacle," I replied, perhaps more wistfully than I intended. "I have spent my life stuck to dream's bottom." And I sighed.

"Our dreams, *Fröschlein*," K said, her mood deepening, "are islands. Floating worlds. But just as certain poisons pass through the protective membrane of the brain, so Trauma infects our dreams, transforming those islands of Paradise into infernal regions, the Hell of nightmare." With a sweeping gesture of the arm indicating the fading light of day she added: "Who breathes overhead in the rose-tinted light may be glad."

It was true that I was breathing in the rose-tinted light of evening, alive, awake, very much awake, my mind looping like a kite – and glad. As we spoke quietly together, the vocal cords of water frogs collided and rebounded in the air.

CHAPTER

I

What is the sea for the man who has loved and left her? She is fire-water, whisky, rum, a roric flame. She is a green-eyed witch; she speaks in tongues. Her coral rings are forged of skeletons; her white shoulders glisten with the dust of powdered bones.

She is memory, the number of numbers, the eye of the world, the mirror of the sea. What is the ocean for the sailor who has loved and left her? The one lover who dissolves the night. A bottomless glass of moonshine.

And sailors? All sea-talkers. The sons of mermen.

Totor was more than a man; he was the perpetual glamour of the sea made flesh. Master of foam, of fish, of dancing ships, with humour and sadness (this aged shellback, landlocked in retirement, missed the sea), he told of opal mists and listing ships, the stuff of tears and wonder which took root in the flood lands of my curiosity and made me as sensitive to the marvellous as a jellyfish is to the sunlight.

Totor was a wolf, a sea-wolf; he stalked stories as an octopus stalks prey: goggle-eyed, on tippy-toe, funny and ominous. Son of a flat-fish! He'd curse sailor, he'd curse salty. Son of a Hindoo whore! Son of a gun, small fry, pass the cider!

And with a wind-chapped hand he'd pour out two foaming mugs of liquid amber before launching into yet another tale.

As Totor speaks, curly-bearded Odysseus lumbers into the room to listen, and sea elephants, and Sindbad – the sinister Old Man of the Sea still clinging to the scruff of his neck. Many times do I, set to float upon the pure waters of Totor's love, nod off upon his knees, the quicksilver of his words spilling me to sleep. Starboard, I swear I hear the surf beating against the window-pane. I sleep in a room carpeted with sand.

In the late afternoons I awake from my nap, the house gently throbbing like a heart against my heart, bathed in the milky haze of the aquarium (for the windows are all paned in green glass), the sun of day receding along the floor like a woman's skirts, the air basted in the sweet smells of Other Mother's kitchen: melted butter, caramel, pigeons swaddled – like playthings or presents – in vine leaves, and seized in a gay fire.

Quick as a hazel-hen, Other Mother, her skin smelling of roses and her apron of starch, busies about her hearth among the silver laughter of her cutlery, her white dishes beached on her shelves like shells. I sit on Totor's knee in the green honey of the room, watching coals crumble to ashes, and listen to pigeons singing in their jackets. Totor pulls out his tobacco pouch from his pocket and prises the shavings with fingers so sea-worn they no longer have prints. Outside, hail spatters on the glass and the room is plunged into darkness. Other Mother hurries to light the lamps and the prodigious promise of our supper is set out upon the table. For dessert she has made a floating island.

Here is the heartbeat of the house: the tidewater of light and darkness, a deepening green, a kindly knee, the smell of gravy and roses. God's own rain falls upon Totor's house; the firmament is his, twilight and the moon. The house sops up stories like a sponge; the beams and rafters, heavy with adventure, creak. Other Mother is up to rise the sun; mornings, I too rise eagerly.

Other Mother opens her kitchen door wide, flooding the room with all the smells of a summer's night: flowering hyssop, sage, the sorrel patch, which threatens to invade our back stoop, gull flight (I swear their feathers leave a sweet smudge upon the air), the seaweed tumbled on the nearest beach, the water itself, yes, the sea. . . . The smell of sea water fills the house.

Drifting, I lie and listen to the waking city. Other Mother teases me out of bed with the sound of butter churning and a song about a stick, a cabbage, and a hole in the ground. Hypnotic, more bedtime than waking song, it is a fitting song for churning, too. There is much to do with walking in circles, digging a circular hole in the ground, prodding it with a stick and circling back again after dark to shoo away rabbits, beggars, and thieves – the Devil's own disguises. And now I hear birdsong, the market criers, and fresh milk splashing in the pan. Before my shirt is tucked into my breeches I am downstairs, barefoot; and before you can count to four, blowing into coffee so hot it has been known to melt a pewter spoon.

I stir in milk, making circles, planting lullaby cabbages, and dig into a piece of bread the size of a shoe. Her fresh butter hits the roof of my mouth like lightning.

"If I was a pig," I tell her, "I'd roll in this butter."

"If you was a pig, you most certainly would not!"

"Why can't people churn butter with their feet?" Her answer is to push a dish of apricots beneath my nose. I lick the coffee from my spoon and plunge it, still hot, into the fruit. It tastes like Other Mother has gone and stewed the sun.

Other Mother has her own stories to tell. She joined the Captain's household in 1883 – and this would be the man who discovered –

"The New Hebrewdees or some such. A mere girl I was, no bigger than the Pope's nose. I learned all I know from the cook, one Madame Pittance, a cut-the-gills-and-don't-slouch sort of a person, proud of her culminary talents – as well as she had a right to be – who instructed me in the arts of cookery and related matters: herbaldry, marketing, pickles, and what have you. A stout woman, this was, not to say obese, and when at fifty she succumbed to auricular ataxia – and it was I who found her headfast in the vinegar barrel and never have I, Heaven help us, seen such various veins (how she must have suffered yet gave no wind of it), I was dramatically propulsed from scullery to kitchery. I hired a miniature *Parisienne*, old as my shoes but nevertheless up to snuff, to scull in my stead.

"I started off with pan-ash. For her birthday, Prince Osky had sent Madame –"

"Prince Osky?"

"His monkeyer. Name was something unpronounceable and posh – Obelnosky, Obbezotsky – so we just referred to him as Old Osky, not that he was *old*, mind you."

"What was his monkey like?"

"His monkeyer. His nickname in other words. Old Osky didn't curry flavour with monkeys. Had no pets of any kind. Kicked Madame's screwbald dog whenever he got the chance. (On the other hand, he always played the gentleman with Madame.)

"Old Osky'd sent a jar of Castilian caviar – that's to say the overlys of fish – which was served the following Sunday. Abbé Whatsis was invited – and I knows that Monsieur L'Abbé was unordinarily fond of my eggplant pancakes. So I served the overlys with those and it occurs to me after, when I was blessed to find a greengrocer who could provide the ecstatic avocado, that the next time we should receive the overlys, I should serve them nesting in halves. This I was able to do sooner than expected, for once Madame had written to Old

Osky describing my fancy, he, ever the galantine, *sends yet another* jar by courier! (And this courier courted me but failed to win my heart; those days I was too busy pleasing Madame to be pleasing men.)"

Other Mother's summer months were spent by the sea. . . .

"In a pink villa. The kitchen was small but sunny and a minute's walk to market where everything that swims was up for action. I was able to prepare such dedicacies as turbot sauced with burnt butter – a nice, light supper if served with a crisp green salad."

And it was in the summer of 1887 that she was "courted and sedated" by a sailor who sported a tattoo, the only vulgar thing about Totor.

"On a rare afternoon of liberty, the pantry well stocked for the captain's evening meal (I had prepared potted tongue, potted eel, potato salad, and peeled tomatoes), I met Totor at the seaside fair. Up and up we went in that insomnic device the ferret wheel; I half expected my heart to run away with itself, instead it ran away with Totor. After, we fell head over heels in love over a terrarium of mussels (and to this day I always add tarragon to mine, although sometimes I do them in saffron, which is lively too)."

"Where is Totor's tattoo?" I ask. Rose blushes and falls silent. I cannot get another word out of her all afternoon.

On Sunday dressed for church, Other Mother smells of pepper. "My splendour!" Totor calls her. "My fat pullet. My own Rose." And she: "Pig!" because he's pinched her. But Totor is more an eel or a quick, yellow fish with a tongue of fire and turquoise eyes. He is small, shorter than Rose, but he carries himself loose and square-shouldered like a man twice his size. Every step Totor takes is a step taken in grace. Sometimes you'd think he floats – so even his stride, so even-tempered the man. Thinking of him now, my heart pulses like a full-fed river.

"God bless Other Mother," says Totor as we walk down to the port and our little boat *La Georgette*, "she doesn't make us go to church. I can't bear to be anywhere I can't see the sky; I can't abide the church air's sickly hue, that everlasting smell of foggy, foggy dew! Besides, I figure that God is nowhere near that featureless bog they call His House; but Rose insists the prayers 'keep her fit,' and those churchy hours are her only quiet time, though I do believe she goes for the salty taste of gossip she gets after. However, the woman has her own mind and needs to plunge it in Holy Water now and then, else it gets yeasty, or so she says – did I tell you the time?"

For a moment he is occupied untying *Georgette*'s knot. I clamber aboard, seeding bubbles in the thickening water. In less than a minute we are gliding as comfortable as kings, Totor handling the sails and I readying the tackle – today we're eeling. . . .

"Did I tell you the time I saw the Vouivre?"

"The Vouivre!" The Vouivre is a woman and. . . .

"She's amphibious too. She haunts the limpid eyes of the world, Nicolas: oceans, lakes, pools, ponds, and rivers. It is she you hear tapping at the window in the rain and breathing in the rushes by the river bank. She whispers in whirlpools and in the ooze of marshes, crouches in the shadows of drowned logs.

"She is enchantment – a warm-blooded aquatic animal. Crab and girl, serpent and siren – see that froth there? That's her suds; seems she's been up early washing her pretty hair – and see that foam? That's her cream. She's busy mornings, just like Rose, churning. She talks to the fish, knows all the oysters by name. It just may be, unknowingly, that you and I have fished her friends." I look concerned.

"Don't worry, Nini. I have an arrangement with the Vouivre." He winks. "She don't mind we take an eel or two – just as long's we take no small fry and don't get boisterous. She lives a peaceable life."

"Where does she sleep?"

"Makes her bed on the sand beneath the water; just lays down and the snails' conversations put her to sleep. Would you, too! Shellfish haven't all that much to say to one another. And sometimes she sleeps in a room."

"A room?"

"Where the sea has swallowed the land, there are cities carpeted with skulls and iron spoons and coins. The Vouivre ignores the treasure and the bones; currents and the filtered moon interest her more than the riches and destinies of men. If you look well and hard, Nicolas, you may – if you are lucky (and I believe you are) – see her, see her *just once*, for she can't be seen twice, else you pay for your curiosity with blindness or your life. And," he adds out of the blue, "*never* let me catch you pissing in the water. She'll grab you, Nini; she'll pull you in by your impertinence!" I laugh and look up in time to see a hundred clouds sailing in the sky.

If I never miss an occasion to be out on the water beside Totor, I have never caught a fish. I have caught hunks of water-logged driftwood, well-barnacled and black, but the only living thing I've ever caught are blue crabs on the beach and clams. But his prowess is uncanny. Smelts, in their dozens, no bigger than crickets (that Other Mother drowns in batter and deep-fries, and that we gobble down whole, heads and all), long, luminous eels that she stews in wine, tuna sweet as suckling pig.

We eat our Sunday dinner in the dining-room. The doors of frosted glass are closed, muting the kitchen sounds. I admire the sooty paintings of continents announced by breakers, of lonely lighthouses assailed by lightning. We eat the day's take, a dorado stuffed with our stoop's sorrel, Rose rarely sitting but spinning from table to kitchen and cellar, a whirling dervish of domesticity.

"Pig!" Rose's Sunday *décolletage* framed in taffeta and masked in lace excites Totor. And he:

"For God's sakes, *sit down!*" But she has already bustled off.

"There's a bottle to be filched from the pantry and the pie –" Pie! Totor complains: it's plum and she's left in the pits; he swears he'll crack a tooth.

"Or choke. And you'll both be back in church and Nini fatherless twice over –"

"Hush!" There is a moment's embarrassed silence I pretend to ignore.

"You were going to tell me about the time you saw the Vouivre. . . ."

"Ah! She was green but beautiful, Nini, enough to cut your heart-bone to the quick, a singular creature born of the deep's blackest flame. I saw her wading, her hair streaming, and taken by surprise I cried out. Blast it! I startled her!"

"What did she do?"

"She turned and when she saw me, laughed. 'Follow me,' she said, 'if you have the heart.' And she was gone. If I had the heart to follow, son, I swear I didn't have the guts! Not to lie – I was scared!"

"Out of his fits!" Rose cuffs him on the ear.

"And if you see her again?"

"Damned if I do! Turned to stone! Just like the starfish in the pavement. Why, I'd become a shell, hollow and hard; put me to your ear and hear the voices of cuttlefish! Dearest, ever since, I keep my eyes peeled for the smallest peculiarity and should I get a hint of her, I screw them shut fast as fast can, else be struck –"

"Blind as an old puss!"

"Blind as Oedipus, Rose, but never mind."

CHAPTER

2

Our favourite corner of the city, Totor's and mine, is the Ghost Port Bar, a smoke-filled, shadow-spooked hole-in-the-wall no bigger than an oyster on the half-shell. Like Rose's kitchen, its door and window glass are green; Saturdays we leap from one aquarium into another. I'm a little young, at eight, for such a place, or so nags Rose, but the Ghost Port Bar is Heavenly Mystery and Hellish Nightmare too; I could not have stayed away had Rose bribed me with a thousand-egg floating island.

The atmosphere is thick in there and juicy; I must agree with Rose, there is not much oxygen. Down under the tables it smells like stale tobacco and feet and monkey fur, but higher up the air's embalmed with fresh burning "navy cut," the fumes of rum, zinc polish (and the zinc bar gleams in the half-light like the prow of a spanking new clipper), and the proprietress's underarms.

"Her husband," says Rose, "is a foul-tempered hyperbolic." And the victim of bad teeth and black bile. Saturdays she's the Ghost's one queen, leaves him grouching somewhere in the unimaginable dimness of the second storey sucking a rum-soaked rag. I ask Rose: "Why doesn't the Cod have his teeth pulled?"

"What would it change? He's used to sitting on horns." She sees my confusion.

"A saying. Means he's on the spit, *smarting*."

Saturdays I can never quite forget that upstairs the Cod, once a gentleman and a sailor, is *smarting*, while downstairs his wife is laughing with Totor, Toujours-Là, the Marquis, the other men and me.

There are many nice things about the Ghost. Not the least is the chimp who stands in a large cage at the back of the bar, pulling at his fundamentals – a thing I've not done in public since the age of three. To warm things up the Cod's wife lets him weave around the room shaking hands. His hand is hot, his handshake congenial, and his teeth, very fat, oblong, and yellow, look like piano keys.

The chimp's relations with the Cod's wife are rumoured "seditious" by Rose. I ask: "Why suspicious?"

"He does her laundry, even sleeps in her bed and if *that's* not Peruvious!"

"But he sleeps in his cage! I've seen his little nest!"

"I'm just repeating what the people say."

"After church!" Totor cries, losing patience. "The monkey's innocent; his fingernails the proof he's never touched soap. It's Gilles-Gillesbis what keeps the Cod's wife in tune."

"Gilles-Gillesbis and Artistide Marquis!"

"Rose!"

"I'm just rehashing what I've *heard*, Victor!"

"And Totor? Does she take Totor on, too?"

This is the first time I see them fight. I want to cry but I also feel like laughing. It is Rose who runs to the sink, sobbing, her apron thrown over her head. All this is the fault of the Evil, the Heavenly Ghost Port Bar!

"And PETOMANIA!" Rose wails, hiccups, and wails again. It is true. Last week the chimp, wearing a fire helmet of red paper, had snuffed out a candle flame with a fart. "He could have set the place on fire!"

Totor kisses Other Mother tenderly and dries her tears. He says: "Rosie, it was only a small wind. An oyster sneezing makes less wind." Putting his arm around her he coaxes her back to her chair and, patting her hands, continues:

"Once I witnessed a *big* wind!" I'd heard the tale on Saturday.

"Oh, yes!" I cry. "Tell her about the *Dolly Siren!*"

"She was approaching Cape Horn and crawling because the sea was set like a jelly. As I was looking out over the water I saw the most fearsome apparition sliding up from the horizon and spitting sparks –"

"It was a dragon of smoke chasing her tail!" Leaping from my chair I spin across the room, whistling.

"I heard a roar, and with one breath the moon was blown clean from the sky –"

"And the *Dolly Siren* sent up just like an aeroplane!" Despite Other Mother's protests, I climb onto the kitchen table.

"We saw the sea beneath us and men scattered and thrashing and sinking fast. The wind was so bad on deck a sailor was knocked down dead by a sawfish; an orbiting water barrel tore off the boatswain's ear. Meanwhile, in Tunisia it rained anchovies; tar pots fell from the sky in Tasmania; the sun was so cold above Cairo the Egyptians all turned blue. The ship's cat slid off deck, her rats screaming after. The captain's hair turned white –"

"There was icicles hanging from his nose thick as tusks! Did he look like a walrus, Totor?"

"He did. The anchor scraped the peaks of mountains we couldn't see; we heard it tolling like a bell. 'To the hold!' I cried. We stumbled under. A chest broke loose and squashed the chief mate flat. We heard the monster panting after us and chewing the mastheads to shreds. She could smell us, I swear, and her icy breath near froze us dead. Every time she arched her back the *Dolly* pitched and our skulls went slamming; the sounds of breaking bones so bad Cook himself went mad! There was brains –"

"For Heaven's sake!" Rose shrieks, "Enough!"

"I'm coming to the end. . . . There was squids piled up in the forecastle when we was set down again, battered but still floating, all green and more marine than human. Nothing was left of us but a toothful of gutter crusts, shaking and gruelly, not fit – Nini darling, dearest Rose – *to hold a candle to!*"

Totor has told me that long before the city I know and love was built the sea possessed the land. When the waters evaporated the landlocked creatures were so petrified they turned to stone. The paving stones, stuck like puddings with the fossil pentagrams of starfish, prove Totor tells the truth.

Stranded himself, Totor spends these last years of his life liberating the spirit castaways. The landscape of my boyhood is haunted by ghosts armed with tridents, decked with cockles, tooting twisted conches. When it rains, as it often does, I can hear dogfish barking in the thunder, and in lightning clearly see the claws of catfish striking at the body of Heaven. Evenings the alleys are surging with pelicans and tiger-faced sharks. There is a great hunk of shadow looming like a finned camel just behind the courthouse, and, in the sewers, good (and evil) whales.

Once on my way to school I find a ring fallen, Totor tells me, from the body of a fish. I would not have missed a tribe of pious tuna reading psalms as they vanished two by two down Fools' Alley had I been quicker.

"Didn't you see them? *Run*, lad, and look! Hasty! But *hush*!"

The scales, tails, tongues of sea monsters are secreted, then revealed in the shadows of the floating clouds; the smiles of mermen are scattered on the water, and above the doors of houses Totor points out impressions of webbed fingers.

After, dark-finned dwarfs cavort and if I haven't seen them, I have seen where they've kicked up sand. When the light is right, a solitary head, surely Neptune's, looms half-mocking and half-hidden in the parlour. Did nine man-sized mackerel march on their tails in full naval regalia up and down the street three times on my ninth birthday's eve as Totor insists? I do not doubt him; the air smells of mackerel all week.

I believe that spiders are the fishermen of the air, and bluebottle flies the not-so-distant cousins of flying fish. I am visited with the certitude as I lie in bed, that all nature's infinite combinations are divine. That the spirit of the marvellous permeates all things, even, at supper's end, the eel's soft spine coiled upon my dish.

Above the stairwell Totor has painted:

Rejoice! All Things Are Born in Foam!

and inscribed upon the wall above their bed:

Had Rose been finned,
Totor
could not have loved her more.

CHAPTER

3

Saturday and pissing vinegar. The old port has vanished in the rain; port and sky and sea all smeared together like a jam of oysters, pearl-grey and viscous. Our heads bent against the wind, Totor and I make our way to the Ghost and trample in sneezing, arrested by the hot fumet of drinking men and their smoke. The place is packed with faces, some sinister, some sad, some joyous; some slashed, tattooed, marked by frostbite, fever, liquor. Toujours-Là is there, his blue eyes blinking, and Aristide Marquis, and the chimpanzee, his simple face pressed to a mug of punch.

The punch is strong and hot. I get some too, with a nice, fruity slice of lemon peel.

"And nurse it, Nini, go slow. That's sailor stuff, see, made for men equipped with solid copper piping." The Cod's wife slips me a gritty stick of peppermint to stir with; there is monkey hair stuck to the sides.

"And my love is as vast as—" the Marquis moans boozily, and Toujours-Là, through smoke and din cuts in:

"My arse!" Which almost causes an incident. But the Marquis is easily coaxed back into felicity and soon the two are singing together. The Cod's wife joins in fortissimo – leaning over the piano and holding her breasts with both hands – and Totor off-key, with a song, though none of us know it, shamelessly lifted (and scrambled) from Apollinaire:

"... The star above your garter
   as tight as a nut cracker;
   your mouth my delight, my nectar –
   O Lu-Lu! Lu-Lu!"

The tiddly chimp, rocking alone on the floor, but carefully, so as not to spill a drop, quivers with excitement as the Cod's wife sends the song cascading with a voluptuous treble:

"oooh Lu-Lu, Lu-looh!"

Outside the fog is like a fine dust rising. The familiar street surges with shadowy figures before a gust of wind blots it out altogether. Inside, we are all warm and cosy. The place is packed, the air palpable with all that breathing. Toujours-Là and the Marquis leave the piano for a game of dominoes. The chimp and I continue to nurse our punch, sucking drop by drop from our swiftly dissolving sugar sticks. Through half-closed eyes I admire the domino constellations and thrill to the sounds they make as they snap against the table. I lust after Toujours-Là's white clay pipe barely perceived in the semi-darkness; it is shaped like a mermaid with nipples and eyes of gold enamel: they twinkle.

I intuit a connection, perplexing and profound, between those eager eyes and nipples and in those oblong skies of darkest night pierced with planets. The Ghost's constellations mirror those in Heaven.

My head foggy with rum, my mouth swollen with sugar, I imagine holes in the sky through which the sleet comes sliding (a quick glance out the window shows that fog has turned to rain, and rain to ice; the streets are paved with it and outside, drunken men tumble like skittles). We are marooned. The Ghost Port Bar has become our island.

The Cod's wife brings out some herring for supper, boiled

potatoes and slices of bread. The taste of salt herring, hot potato, rum, and bread so good I savour every particle. I do not think of Other Mother anxiously prodding the Sunday roast.

The Marquis has finished eating.

"Toujours-Là," he says, "last Saturday Totor told us a famous story; it started badly but it ended well – the *Dolly Siren* waking in an inlet off the sunny coast of Sumatra and ever sea-worthy despite her detour in the sky. I'd say it's up to you to tell another, but this time start it well and end it in disaster."

Toujours-Là pulls his pipe from his lips and, scratching a jowl, says:

"This story is disastrous from start to finish; no way getting around that." The chimp has fallen asleep on his feet, his body bent in two, his cheek resting on the floor. But I, I begin to wake up.

"I hope it's about a mermaid!" I whisper loudly to Totor. Toujours-Là says:

"Yes, it is. More or less. Yes, it is, hah! *In its way*. But then it isn't, neither." I fear he is asking riddles.

At the other side of the room a few men are leaving; Toujours-Là waits for the scraping of their chairs and the clatter of their clogs to cease. As they go a gust of cold wind slams into the room and the chimp shivers in his sleep.

"Our bloody hulk, the *Annabelle Lee*, had sprung any number of leaks and was forced to dock in the port of an aborted rock pile not fit to be called a city, so ugly it burned the eyes." Toujours-Là begins with a voice like a barrel rolling down a road. "This city was famous for its kilns and crockery. Figurines no bigger than a starving man's turds sat in all the windows. I hated them worse than the bugs which overran the beds.

"I killed time drinking a sooty whisky. The bar's proprietor had a collection of the peculiar pottery – a dozen stood on a shelf, and, as the Devil would have it, were reflected in a mirror, which made them twice as many, as if twelve was not enough, Goddammit, and I was forced to look at twenny-four. I saw bad luck in it. Figured they was telling me I'd be stuck there for as many months. I swallowed the bastard's poison, trying not to inhale, and blasted those clay birdies from their perch with the pistol of my mind.

" 'I see you admiring my collection,' said the arse-hole barkeep. 'Some are very old. These days they ain't so nicely glazed.' He showed me a piece of crap which was supposed to be a starfish. I lost my temper and sent it to the floor where it didn't shatter, but rolled with a tinkle that sounded like laughter. He threw me out, but I was eager to go, sick to death of his cursed bric-à-brac damned with nine lives. I was even missing the pissing *Annabelle Lee*.

"Now, this place was known for more than its crockery. I'd heard rumours that a mermaid had been seen swimming in the canal. So I stopped a fella and said: 'Hey! Where's this mermaid I've heard about?'

" 'A myth!' he lisped. 'A fairy-tale!' But shame hid his eyes like slime. He was lying. 'A myth! Make believe!'

"I roughed him up, which was easy. He was as limp as a dead snake. He begged for pity and insisted he had *nothing to do with it*."

The room is quiet; everyone is listening to Toujours-Là. The only sound is the chimp's gentle snoring. The Cod's wife is standing between Toujours-Là and the Marquis, one hand on Toujours-Là's shoulder, the other playing with a lump of amber the Marquis has hanging from his neck.

" 'You're lying!' I yelled. 'I want to see her! Take me to her!' He fell down sprawling. I was drunk, evidently. I pulled him up by the ears.

" 'No!' he sobbed. 'She'll kill me!'

" 'Who?' I said, giving him a slap. 'Who? *Who?*' But in a sudden frenzy he kicked me in the shin and scuttled off.

"The night swallowed him whole. I walked on, shadows thieving around me. I lost my way. An hour went by and I didn't know where the Hell I was. I walked into puddles and I stepped on something queer; I lost my matches and my shin was hurting. Then I felt someone tugging at my pants – a dwarf. He came up to my knees. Said he knew a place where we can get island rum. For a drink he'll tell me all I want to know.

"We went off together, the dwarf tugging at my pants, first this way, then that. Then I saw a bright light shining – a place what calls itself the Scheherezade. I set the little fellow up with a bowl of flaming punch the size of a sink. I know Heaven exists, Nini! It's that place – the Scheherezade.

" 'She was born a beauty,' the dwarf began, wiping his lips with his wrist like a gentleman, 'perfect to the nails of her toes, dancey, all sparkle, a little fairy-child, truly. When her mama died her father married a diabolical female, happy only when she heard bones breaking beneath her shoes. A witch this was, dim-witted. Liked to smash roaches between her thumbs. A calamity, really, not a woman. More a precipice. When the old fool died of melancholy she savagely mutilated the child. Cut off her hands and feet and cauterized the wounds with fire.' "

Totor cries: "Toujours-Là! Nini's just a boy!" I kick him, not wanting to be babied. Toujours-Là continues:

"Now when the child's wounds was healed, the ghoul threw her into the canal. Set her to paddle as best she could with her lopped-off limbs. 'And so she lived,' the dwarf said to me, 'like a pale carp of nightmare. Like a pale carp of nightmare bobbing for crusts.'

"That's how the stories began: bargemen sometimes saw the yellow hair, her white bottom as she dove after her dinner, poor angel, and no one doing a thing. Too scared of the ghoul. But the dwarf looked for her until he found her. And when he had some supper he slipped down to the water and shared it. Because she was so afraid he could never get near, he'd toss her a peeled chestnut, an onion. He said her skin was scaly and her hair gone green.

"The Scheherezade was closing. The dwarf took me back to his dismal room. He lived in a cellar by the port. It smelled of tar. I was surprised to see no furniture, not even a pallet of straw: only packing crates and all of them empty.

" 'I tamed her,' the dwarf continued, 'although it took time. I wrapped her in my threadbare coat and brought her here. All night I kissed her and held her and rocked her. I sang the little scraps of songs I remembered. I promised her dolls with wee cabinets. At dawn she smiled, a dazzlement, and gasping like a fish she died. I fear she died of too much tenderness. And now she haunts the city. Just as I do myself.'

"The dwarf had come to the story's end. Dawn dispelled the night. To my surprise, I saw that as the shadows lifted he dwindled.

" 'The Ogress,' he spluttered as he vanished, 'the Ogress found me and now. . . .' His voice was a diminishing trickle. 'I haunt the night like a candle. Days I die. . . . Thanks for listening. . . .' I could barely hear him. 'I hope we'll meet again. . . .' "

"A ghost!" I gasp. Totor squeezes my knee. Toujours-Là continues:

"I stumbled out into the mazes of the streets until I found myself back at the first bar. The infernal pottery nodded at me just as if we shared a secret. . . ."

My mouth drops.

"Now, Nini," says Toujours-Là, all at once concerned, "don't have any nightmares on me. The story was the fault of Master Punch and no reality. The Ogress but a figment of my addled brain."

But the sailor's apologies and explanations only convince me the tale is true. The story of the maimed maiden has struck a deep and sonorous chord in my heart. Never have I been so famously entertained, nor so frightened.

Outside the sleet is transformed to a heavy fall of snow. The chimp licks a domino and tries to stick it to his nose. I suck my candy thoughtfully.

"Tell me about the Ogress!" I plead. "What happened to her?"

Totor sighs. "I fear, old salt," he says, "my stories pale beside your own."

"I've never been so scared!" I admit. "I could tell the tale is true!"

"Hah! My truth," Toujours-Là insists, "is whisky's. Son, my brain is yellow like Hook Head in the moon and not always navigable. My tales, boy," he spits, "are born in puddles of rum."

"And that," the black Marquis cries, "is the truth!" Is Toujours-Là about to cry? Just then two tears, like yellow grapes, roll off his nose.

Dressed in the Cod's tassellated nightcap the chimp rocks over and seizes my hand. He looks like a little person in the cap. He lays his head down upon my knees. The feel of his furry face and its surprising warmth is, like the tepid punch and the soft fall of snow, delicious.

"The Ogress!" I insist. "What happened to *her*?"

"I heard," Toujours-Là whispers, setting a flame to his pipe and sucking hard, "that someone tied a rock around her neck and threw her into the canal."

"It was you!"

"Not so fast, son – you're as fast as planets, *whoosh*!" He makes a circle in the air with his thumb.

"She's dead!"

"I saw a face once in the Arctic, shining white in the black water. A woman's face, following in the ship's wake, following fast. And *angry*, Nini; with eyes of phosphorus. I figured she was after me."

"Brrr! And since?"

"Oh, since. . . ." He sends the Cod's wife to the bar for a finger of whisky for everyone but me.

"Could someone swim like that in the icy water?"

"Not *someone*, Nini. Like I said – this was a calamity. She was without a body – just a lonely head bewitched, riding the inky foam after my sanity. Her head was like a ball of ice with eyes, intent on doing harm."

I shudder, enraptured.

"I saw the head again off Bloody Foreland, but – it's the Marquis' turn to tell a tale."

"Something romantic," Totor hastily proposes, "else the lad get warped notions of the fair sex." For this he gets another kick. I will not be babied!

"Cool down," Totor says to me, "the night has just begun." Meaning I'll be up very late, and this salves my bruised dignity. "Though," he adds under his breath, "Rose will bread our ears."

I look up. The windows of the Ghost Port Bar are crusted with ice and the world beyond extinguished. To myself I breathe: "Hook Head! Bloody Foreland!"

CHAPTER

4

Around his strong, black neck, the Marquis wears a knob of amber knotted to a blue string. Catching my eyes fixed to his throat he lifts it to my face and I see, caught like a seal in Arctic ice, a tiny, grey bee. My astonishment amuses him and he laughs broadly, straining the spindly body of his chair. I ask:

"Have you been to Hook Head and Bloody Foreland, too?"

"Ah!" he says warmly, in his voice of cinnamon. "I've been to Bûr Sa'id, Shāhbāzpur, and Hooghly, Crooked Island, Easter Island; I've been to Corpus Christi." To my delight he repeats this in song:

"I've been to Bûr Sa'id,
   Shāhbāzpur and Hooghly,
   Crooked Island, Easter Island;
   I've been to Corpus Christi."

Then, bending over imaginary oars, the Marquis rows himself right out of his chair and around the room in an invisible boat which dips and rises, dips and rises, dips and topples over. Holding his nose, he tumbles extravagantly into deep water, and sinks. He surfaces, spitting, and shading his eyes as if from the sun, peers about until he sees me. When he does, he waves madly and paddles over to my chair where, on bended knees, hunched and breathless, he raises the amber sphere to the level of my eyes and both gentle and mocking, whispers:

"Does Tit-Nini
love my bee?
Her name is
Tit-Erzulie."

I blush with pleasure. I have never met anyone like the
Marquis.

"Listen! Listen! Tit-Z'oreilles . . . Tit-Erzulie is telling you
a *story; buhz . . . buhz . . . buhzzzzzzzzzzzz!*" He holds the
sphere to my ear. I could swear I hear the bee humming very
softly.

"It's magic!"

"Everything, Tit-Z'oreilles, is magic." He springs into the
air and, grabbing a phantom cane, executes an engaging soft-
shoe before shuffling over to his chair and sitting down.

"I've seen the sea swarming with painted turtles; a sky so
full of flying fish the face of the moon was veiled for hours.
These fish whistled as they flew, and because, like parrots,
they repeated everything they overheard, recited verses from
the Koran, the Bible, and even *Moby Dick*. Imagine, Tit-
Nini," and he fingers the bead as he speaks, "imagine a thousand thousand fish flying in the sky and all crying out at once:

"There is one God and His name is Allah!
O how beautiful is my beloved. Her eyes are
doves and her lips a scarlet ribbon!
Of all divers, thou hast dived the deepest!"

And yes, I can imagine it.

Toujours-Là raps his pipe angrily against the table:

"Out with it, Marquis!" he cries. "Cease this convoluted
foot-scraping at the door, this perambulatory –"

The Cod's wife arrives with more punch steaming in a
pewter pitcher. Stroking the Marquis' handsome face she
sighs:

"It's not every man goes in for the perambulatories." The

Marquis brushes her hand away as if it were a fly. I ask who Allah is. Is he any relation to the old fogey in the sky Rose calls Gee-hover: He who Hovers Over?

"One and the same! Cursing folks with boils and brimstone. Now, boys, my perambulations are nearly over, but not quite. There's a bit more. That is to say *if you don't mind*." He looks at me and his tiger's eyes twinkle. The amber sphere glows against the deepest nightshade of his skin like a planet in space.

"Oh! No! Not at all! I don't mind at all!" Despite the hour I've forgotten to be sleepy. My belly full of herring and my mind alive with talking fish and the humming bee, I'm wild for another tale and jiggle impatiently in my chair.

"My ancestors were traders in gold and ivory and wax," the Marquis continues. "They bought and sold madder and rose water, quicksilver, and gold on strings. They knew all the bright sapphire ports of Africa's eastern seaboard; they sailed the swiftest ships the world had ever seen – from Sofala to Mozambique, to Ras Hafun and even to Ceylon." Taking a turquoise pencil from his pocket, he lightly draws a map of mediaeval East Africa on the oily table-top, including the ancient city of Zimbabwe, the Congo, the Nile, India, Ceylon, and the great island of Madagascar which hangs on the sea like a shattered tear. He draws ruffled mountains, fulmigating volcanoes, forests and deserts, and even a black wind whipping up from Cape Horn and roaring across the Indian Ocean.

"They bartered with Persians and Chinese and Arabs; they brought jade from China into Africa; some worshipped Allah, some Gee-hover, some wedded the women of the Sabea, some settled in Ceylon where the girls are as graceful as gazelles. King Solomon himself traded with my ancestors. His throne was built of their ivory; he ate fruit from their ebony tables and the peacocks –"

"You're bragging!" Toujours-Là growls. "And the tale's too flow'ry. Nothing is happening, just a lot of twitteration.

Gazelles! Peacocks! Ivory! Thish ish the twentieth century an' we don't give two hoots for your ancestors – all niggers too!"

"I do! I do!" I cry, startled by this outburst.

"Ah! Maybe Toujours-Là is right, Nini," the Marquis says gently. "All that's gone. Frozen in the past like my bee Erzulie. My ancestors, their blue cities clustered like blossoms, their oceans, and the blazing candles of their ships, their charts set with stars, their latitudes and longitudes of knotted gold, their joyous feasts and their deep, cool wells. . . . Now nothing remains but the silent, dusty hills tufted with scree and graves raked over by antiquaries. My people have become scavengers, without boats, without dreams, tending fires of thorn, fires of dung. They eat locusts. They die of thirst."

"But why?"

"Slavery, Little Ears. Africa's Black Death."

"Tragedy's everywhere," says Toujours-Là. "Your people was not the only ones to know hard times. My ancestors was serfs for Kings. They lived on beans. Generations living on beans why I'm so squat. The braggart has always got to sell his soup first," he says to me under his breath. "He's too proud of his hoity-toity forefathers and I always steal a snooze, if I can, during his peram –"

"My grand-daddy," the Marquis continues, as he rubs out the map of Africa with the palm of his hand, smearing his skin with lead, "was the last in a long line of seamen. Pity those who have nothing left, Tit-Nini; pity those whose luck has run out. He was a Haitian nigger, that blackest of blacks, and the grandson of a slave. All he ever had was a leaky boat and some weevilled sugar cane to sell for the manufacture of rotten rum. And even that he lost."

"All my grand-daddy every had was beans!" Toujours-Là insists.

"Come on," Totor complains, "let the Marquis talk. What's come over you?"

"It's liquor makes me mean," Toujours-Là admits. "But the

nigger repeats himself. I've heard this pro-long of his before and so has you."

"Nini hasn't," Totor reminds him.

"This noble nigger likes to take his time," the Marquis says with an easy laugh. "Time's about all I have."

"We've got all night!" I cry, squeezing Totor's hand under the table. "Haven't we, Totor!"

"All night."

"All night!" thunders Toujours-Là. "I can't take another minute. I'm up to my ears in the black man's blue blood; I swear to God I'm drowning!" And to the Cod's wife, he mumbles, "Come, slut, give ush a kish!"

"I'll give you a *kick*!" she scolds, and she does; she kicks the seat of his chair. "Get out. You're ruining everybody's time." Her most queenly, she points to the door.

"I," he says as with difficulty he pulls himself to his feet and weaves his way across the room, "was jus' going." He stumbles out into the snow.

"BEANS!" we hear him cursing, "BEANS! BEEEANS!"

"He's just so jealous," the Cod's wife shrugs her shoulders and gazes upon the Marquis with tenderness. "He's getting old."

"He'll freeze out there," the Marquis says. "He'll freeze his arse out there!"

"He needs to cool off," says Totor, mildly.

"He's melting the snow off the stoop." The Cod's wife strokes the lobe of the Marquis' ear. He pulls his head away. "He's sitting down," she adds.

"The bastard will catch pneumonia," the Marquis insists. Totor agrees:

"I'll go fetch him."

Just then Toujours-Là staggers back in. "A man could die out there!" he sputters, colliding into the Cod's wife and nearly knocking her over. "Sweet Mother!" he says, holding on to her as she batters his chest with her fists. "You smell good, like crude oil . . . like cold tobacco. . . . Angel, you smell like fish, *cod* fish!" Laughing bitterly he pushes her away.

"I'm worried about him," says Totor. "I've never seen him quite like this before."

"If I were a lesser man," says the Marquis, "why *Goddammit*, I'd –"

Just then there is a frantic pounding on the ceiling overhead; it is the Cod.

"Throw the buggers out!" he screams. "It's way past midnight."

"Time to go," the Cod's wife caresses my hair apologetically. "Forgive him – his piles –"

"ARE SOME OTHER BUGGER'S UNIVERSE!" Toujours-Là shouts as he scrambles after a bottle. "THE ENTIRE GALAXY'S JUS' SOME POOR BASTARD'S BLEEDIN' –"

"For God's sake – someone shut him up!" the Cod's wife pleads. I say:

"He must be smarting *bad* to shout like that! Hey! Aren't we going to hear the Marquis' story?"

"Rose must be in a lather, Nini!" Totor slaps my behind. "Come, darling, we're off!" The Marquis slams his glass down on the table as do I, first fishing out the twist of rind I've been saving for the road.

Gingerly we step out into the night, the Marquis navigating Toujours-Là who has gone limp. The Ghost Port Bar stands smoking in the snow. The Cod barks, the Cod's wife cuts the lights, and we wave goodbye in the dark.

Totor and I thread home. Beneath the porch light our swept path appears like a valley of diamonds.

CHAPTER

5

Other Mother is up, tying knots in her apron and wringing her hands. Her lower lip quivers when I kiss her.

"Ah! Rose!" Totor says much too loudly. "Forgive your wayward men! But it was sleeting fishes!"

"And I! And I!" she whines. "Sitting on pins and nettles! Did you think for one minute of the meat? A frugal cut but well prepared – and the potatoes – ruined!"

"We thought, we *longed* for it, Rosie, but we was marooned at the Ghost. We are as hungry as hounds," he lies, "so slice it, dearest; let's have a midnight feast – why, truly, it could be Christmas, see – we've tracked in snow!" She melts. Body and soul, Rose leans towards the pantry.

"We have pickles?" I pick up Totor's ploy, although stuffed to the gills. Rose will never know the extent of our heroism, which is really just another shape our love for her sometimes takes.

"Pickles! Before sleep!" Our Rose has forgiven us entirely. "I *thought* you might be late," she admits, "so I made a mayonnaise." Head bowed, she runs to fetch it.

"The Marquis was there!" I shout after, "and Toujours-Là!" Rose clucks her tongue. She has forgiven us and is pleased to be feeding us, but she does not approve of the company we keep. With a smart thud, she sets down a bowl. The mayonnaise is deep yellow; pearls of moisture glisten on the top. Just looking at it makes me queasy. As my stomach reels, Other

Mother's crockery slides past the corner of my eye. Some uncanny influence grabs the kitchen by the face and twists its familiar features out of shape. I feel at once so forlorn that it comes to me, drunk as I surely am and giddy from lack of sleep, that this is the wrong house and dearest Rose, with her red, swollen face, crumpled apron, and beetling brows, an imposter. Had I been bitten by a viper I could not have felt stranger; I am tormented by a mad desire to laugh at the sudden poverty of Rose's bottled eggs, her cherries in vinegar, the brash, bare bellies of her copper pots; her efforts to create order in what Toujours-Là had that very hour exposed as a riotous universe.

Set out on the undulating surface of Other Mother's table the faience salt and pepper shakers in the shape of windmills look like martyred thumbs. The white dishes, lovingly soaped and dried, shine too brightly and it occurs to me that a knife can be used for more than slicing cold roast beef. I Shudder. Other Mother, who misses nothing, raves: "He's caught his death!" I begin to cry.

Is death so catching? She puts her lips to my temples and with her freckled nose nuzzles after fever. "He reeks of rum!" Spinning about, she glowers at Totor. "Victor! If you ever – if you *ever* take the boy back to that, that *din of pernickety* . . . it will be over my dead body!"

Startled, I look up at Totor with disbelief. My eyes dry up at once. What have I done? I have brought upon this catastrophe by behaving like a baby. I do my best to pull myself together, but the table refuses to co-operate and the little bowl of mayonnaise swells to the outsize proportions of the soup tureen she uses twice a year to moat her *cotriade*.

"I'm just – I'm terribly sleepy, is all; and I'm not hungry, Other Mother – I –"

"You've eaten her herring, haven't you!" When I look at Totor helplessly, I give us both away.

"Rosie!" he pleads. "We was marooned!"

"I wouldn't touch her herring with a twelve-foot pole!" shouts Other Mother.

"It's all right!" I cry bravely. "Our piping's solid copper!" I cough as heartily as I can to disguise a hiccup, nearly choking on a bubble of gas. "What's a *galaxy*?" I ask, attempting to change the subject.

"Another low-class bar!" Rose shrieks. "Don't tell me you was there too?"

"No! No!" With exaggerated flourish, Totor spears a slice of overcooked meat with his fork. "Toujours-Là was talking about stars –" He pours salt out onto the table.

"Bad luck!" Rose disapproves.

"This is our galaxy, the Milky Way," Totor sweeps the salt across the table with his hand, "and this speck's the sun. The whole caboodle is spinning, see –" I read order and disorder in the turmoil of salt, the spiral galaxies Totor engenders and, with splayed fingers, sets circling in endless revolutions.

"Bringing disaster upon our household!" Rose crosses herself as I, from a vertiginous height and, seeing the universe forming just beneath my nose, am filled with dread and enchantment, ecstasy and fever. I shudder again.

"Get him to bed at once!" Rose commands, "while I boil up some camomile. . . . Herring and rum! Herring and rum!" she incants as Totor lifts me from my chair and takes me into his arms, a thing he has not done in a very long time.

As he climbs the stairs, Totor wheezes. The stairwell is dark and ominous and like everything else tonight, not quite familiar. When he pauses for breath on the landing, a sob escapes me.

"My precious!" he cries, "what is it?"

"The face of the Ogress!" I hide my eyes against his heart.

"It's the moon, Nini! Shining in at the window." In the winter sky, the moon rises like a sharp, silver disc. "Toujours-Là told a scary story, but none of it was true!" For the second time that night I burst into tears, knowing better. As I cannot be comforted, nor, despite the hour, sleep, Rose, having brought up the camomile, returns with another oil lamp and, setting it down before the mantel mirror, tidies up, stooping into the corners as if to exorcize the zoomorphic shadows she has herself provoked by bringing so much firelight into the room. Peeping out from under the covers I see flamboyant scorpions dancing on the walls.

Other Mother dives for my shoes. Totor exclaims:

"Don't they look like turtles in the dark!" Rose prods the wormy laces.

"Is the moon still shining?" Totor goes to the window and lifts the curtain.

"The sky is black, Nini."

"Black," says Rose, "as magic." As I recall, it is at this precise moment that the little iron doorbell rings.

"Who can it be?" Rose complains. "It's nearly two!" Her hands fluttering at her sides, she bounces downstairs. In an instant Totor and I hear the hot-cocoa voice of the Marquis explaining he'd seen the lamps lit and asking if "Tit-Nini's not too grogged up on rum."

"I'm *fine*!" I yell, suddenly better. "Come up! Come up!"

"The poor sausage can't sleep," says Rose as she leads the Marquis up the stairs. "You men have behaved unseasonably. I've never seen Nini so commotioned, and I swear –"

"Aristide."

"I swear, Archimedes, he's not going back there, not ever, not after this! *Not over my dead body!*"

"Oh stop that!" Totor is exasperated. "Stop this talk of dead bodies. You sound like a Yankee funeral parlour!" Rose has never heard of such a thing.

"A place," the Marquis explains, "where they keep the corpses tidy."

"Where's Toujours-Là?" I ask.

"In the arms of Morpheus." Rose frowns at this indiscretion.

"Tell me about that island – that *Easter* Island!"

"Well . . . there were no chocolate chickens anywhere, if that's what you're wanting to know. No pretty eggs in baskets. But there were plenty of *baked* chickens – the Easter Islanders wrapped them in nice new banana leaves and cooked them in deep holes filled with burning stones."

"That's no way to cook!" Rose is scandalized.

"That said, Madame Rose, and not wanting to contradict you – they were the best damned chickens I ever ate anywhere. You see, they baked like that all day slow as snails, and the banana leaves gave them a heavenly savour."

"Sounds good!" I cry. "Doesn't it sound *good*, Totor?"

"You come here this Sunday for supper, Aquarius," says Rose, her vanity piqued, "and I'll show you what I can do with a chicken. And I assures you, Aladdin, I don't need a hole; I swear to God I don't need *stones*, and I don't need, Heaven help me, banana leaves! I was baking chickens long before you was a mere driblet of lard, son – I'm over fifty! And I bakes 'em any and all ways. Why I can bake 'em in ways you couldn't count if you got up early last Thursday, for example: stuffed with lemons and onions, stuffed with sorrel, stale bread, liver and garlic, or parsley, ground pork and veal; larded with bacon, rubbed with pepper – you like pepper?" He nodded. "It entrances the flavour."

"I am entranced," the Marquis beams. "You bake me a chicken and this spring on the first sunny Sunday, I'll take you to a place called Paradis and the best restaurant I know." Rose blushes and reflects.

"Did they bake bananas along with the chickens?" she asks.

"They did."

"It could be good . . . peculiar, but . . . good," Rose concedes. "After all, I've stewed my rabbits with prunes."

"Marquis!" I suddenly remember. "Your story!"

"Hm . . . I know a story about a girl who gets turned into a street lamp."

"A street lamp!" Rose is incredulous. "I've heard of a girl turning into a tree – as I recall she was a geek."

"That girl," says Totor, "was a Greek."

"Anyway," says the Marquis, "that's just one of the many stories I know. But it's not the one I was going to *tell*."

"Could you tell that one now?"

"It's a story that can't be told, Tit-Nini. It's a story without ears. For *eyes*, in other words."

"But it's so late!" Rose kneads her hands helplessly.

"Hush!" Totor says gently, taking her hands into his. "Hush, Rose!"

The Marquis pulls off his socks and, with the ease of a serpent, uncoils from the foot of my bed where he has been sitting cross-legged and as still as a finely carved Buddha of ebony. One and then the other, he places his naked feet down upon the floor, and as the air turns into thicker, mutable stuff, he grows gills, webbed fingers, and fins. Slowly, slowly he wades across the deepening waters of my room, first up to his ankles, then his knees, his loins, his heart. When the waters reach his chin, the Marquis, with a curiously radiant smile (a smile which one day Venus Kaiserstiege will recognize as the same as on the face of La Clarté in the gardens of Versailles as she lifts the morning star to the sky), tosses back his head and sinks beneath his hallucinated ocean to explore those subaqueous cities Totor has described to me so many times, springing the captive spirits I know are always there waiting.

The illusion is so perfect we see bubbles rising from his nostrils, the shoals of tiny shrimp he sweeps with liquid fingers from his eyes. When the weird shadow of an undulating squid slides across the walls, Rose gasps. Pushing up from the ocean floor the Marquis surfaces, and as the waters dissolve, he reaches out and appears to pluck something from Rose's open mouth.

Captivated, I see that he is soaked to the skin, that his hair, dark as grapes, is wet and his face pearled with moisture.

Approaching my bedside he opens his hand and there, shining in the firelight, is Erzulie.

When he slips the blue string over my head I throw my arms around him and kiss him fiercely on the mouth – so thrilled my teeth are chattering. Totor has his arms about Rose, who stands transfixed and staring into the evaporated promise of an evanescent world.

Later, alone, I hear church bells muted by a fresh fall of snow: one, two, three. Rose calls snowflakes meteors, which is confusing. Sleet, hail, rain, snow – all *meteors*, all *planets*. In my damp hand I hold Erzulie, asleep in her planet of amber. Amber is an enchanted substance. Once it has touched the skin it radiates heat. Erzulie warms my hand; the sphere feels soft and silky, and the blue string exudes a faint smell of sandalwood and more: the subtle smoke of the Marquis' skin. I imagine that concealed in the shadows of owl-light the Marquis is sitting at the stern of my bed, my boat; that tonight he is my helmsman.

I have memories of other blizzards, other storms, the sky shuddering and booming, the rain battering the roof and spilling from the gutter onto the street: "The Devil is whipping his daughter! See how she weeps!" as when on an evening I play up in the attic among the "floating Sams" Rose will not allow downstairs – those mysterious objects, all musty, Totor has brought back home from everywhere.

> For I've been to Bûr Sa'id
> Shāhbāzpur and Hooghly;
> Crooked Island, Easter Island
> I've been to Corpus Christi.

Many years from now, K will point to an image of a falling star and ask:

"Tell me, dearest, what does this make you think of?"

"Me . . . auh –" I will be unable to speak. "Pla –" As tears inundate my cheeks, K will take my hand. Moaning I will sit back and, as clouds in the sky tear past like beasts fleeing from a forest on fire, manage to mutter: "Planets."

Totor has described a fish which is white when the moon increases and black when it wanes. As my dreams: some are white as mother's milk and others black as ink.

Totor has told me that like opium dreams, the dreams of the drowning are a way of dying. A nightmare leads to a sweet, luminous reverie, festive and far too bright – a pipe-dream.

Very often, when I was a tiny child, I would awaken mewling with terror. To quiet me, Rose would sing her song of cabbages and sticks. Once I heard her say: "He remembers." What is it I remember, Rose? Totor?

Totor answers: "We are all rafts adrift, son, splinters on the sea." I don't want to be a splinter. I want to be a man.

"A little small, still, for a man!" Rose caresses my hair.

"But I will grow into a man!" I cry, eagerly, loudly – to banish confusion, the hour's queer edge. Standing on Totor's thighs I crow like a cockerel so that they who look so solemn laugh.

Once I catch Totor weeping. "An old story," he insists, "a shipwreck. I lost a friend. Several in fact." He launches a convoluted drama which just this once I do not believe.

Downstairs the clock chimes in turn: one, two, three. Why this discord between the clock and the bells? The question troubles me. *Bells and planets; meteors and bells.* Words felled in flight when once Rose dropped a spool of thread just outside my door at the moment when I tumbled into sleep. Ever since I need only to turn the charm over in my mind for the suspended gardens of the night to claim me. *Bells and planets, meteors and bells.* . . . A path, obscure and umbrageous, leads to a deep lake; already I see it shimmering beyond the trees.

Yet, despite Erzulie burning in my hand like a little sun and the Marquis' magic, tonight the path falls away and I am sent flying to my knees upon a greasy pavement. I recognize the city Toujours-Là described of filthy brick; the sailor is standing before me, the fog hissing at his heels.

"Breathe deeply, son!" says Toujours-Là, "there's whisky on the wind. It's not a crime to lick your lips." And he sings the Marquis' song, except the words are not the same:

> "For I've been burned
>   shat upon and bloodied
>   torn asunder
>   crucified . . . a corpse –"

"I could tell you – I've seen –"
"Please! Don't tell me what you've seen!" But he ignores me:

> "I've seen the crypts of Egypt
>   catacombs and cromlechs . . .
>   the blue morgues of Africa
>   the black pyres of India
>   the graveyards of America
>   the ossuaries of Spain;
>   I've roamed the world all over
>   from mudhole to cesspool
>   from slaughterhouse to butchery
>   and I've drunk with executioners
>   and I've lain with murderers.
>   For the world all over
>   is slaughter –

"– is a cold, cold sepulchre!" he adds, wheezing. "And the cold," he cries, "is rising!"

We are standing knee-deep in icy water. I climb up his back.

"I am not a little monkey!" I shout, for it seems to me that he has said I am. "I am a man!"

"Too small! Too small for a man! You're a monkey! A little macaque! I've heard –"

"Don't tell me what you've heard!"

> "I've heard epitaphs and elegies
> I've heard the tolling bell
> From Mexico to Ireland
> all the world is Hell."

CHAPTER
6

Christmas holidays had begun and I did not miss the school-room, nor my master whose name was Shelled; rather, Shelled is what we called him. He had been shell-shocked during the Franco-Prussian War and he had never entirely recovered. A man of sixty, he appeared to us as someone archaic, even biblical; there was something terrible about this moody man's yellow face ravaged by tics. In his worst moments he threatened to hurl us through the window; on better days he read us stories from Baudelaire's translation of Edgar Allan Poe. I cherish a vivid recollection of Shelled sputtering *The Gold Bug*, one arm bent at a painfully acute angle across his loosely aproned back and the other holding the book within a hair's breadth of his myopia. Further down the aisle one of the wilder boys had shat directly in his path. Shelled stepped neatly over it without changing his inflection.

This wild, scatological boy was the one friend I had made in school. I admired Maximinole who was older than the other boys and who, unlike me, had "no time for stories." Max was interested only in what he called "real things," liberty and, of course, tormenting Shelled. Fossils in pavement, shadows in fog, the beached frames of unfinished boats prodding the air like the skeletons of whales, the moon hanging in the sky like an evil face were without interest. Planets, meteors, old stones, old shells, old sailors' gibberish – what did they matter? What did they prove? Those starfish I went on about were *dead* things. Once in my zeal to win Max over I had bragged about a piece of rock I had found in the attic. It's one polished face offered a seascape perfect in every detail: grottoes, rising mist, cresting waves, reeling birds. Maximinole hotly insisted the thing was impossible, and in an excess of anger had punched me in the face. My profusely bleeding nose and pained expression were too much for him; Max ran from the schoolyard and never returned. Later I learned that he – in that city of sailors – had apprenticed himself to a baker. Someone had seen the fiery Maximinole at dawn bent in two beneath a fifty-kilo sack of flour. Although he hurt me, I've always felt that I pushed him too far, wanting him to see the world in a way he was unable to. I hate to think that this boy who had so brazenly lowered his drawers in the aisle was doing mule's work for a baker.

Companionless, therefore, on that cold December morning on the edge of Christmas, I set off in the slush – for there was a drizzle to the day and the heavy snows of Saturday night and Sunday morning were sliding off the rooftops and into the gutters with a hiss. I sloshed down the street on the lookout for marbles; I had found two favourites this way: an unusually heavy one made, I think, of hematite and a large one of transparent glass filled with thousands of pin-prick bubbles. Faithful to my habit I walked along with my eyes glued to the ground, my old wool beret pulled down over my ears making me look, I hoped, a little like a pirate. I also wore a pair of wool gloves cut off at the fingers. I did not find any marbles that day, but the sloppy water, oily in places and black, and the lumps of unmelted snow calving like icebergs in the miniature oceans of the street, had me continually dreaming. Such was the enchantment of those floating worlds that I lost all notion of place and time and wandered down to the port where the hulls of the season's deserted *sardiniers* rocked in the icy water with a sorrowful, sucking sound. Their names were marvellous: *The Free Thought, Hook's Slave, La Communarde*. Soon the wind sent me scurrying back to the protection of the streets where a thin mist followed me everywhere. The sun was already waning when, with a shiver of foreboding and delight, I recognized the side-street and the alley leading to the Ghost Port Bar. In an instant I saw the Ghost's familiar fogged panes, its ancient stone doorsteps all puddled in the middle.

To the small boy I was, the Ghost inspired awe. I pushed the door open and entered on tiptoe. At first I could see nothing but the bottles twinkling like precious stones behind the bar: the hot ice of *eau-de-vie*, kirsch, and kümmel, absinthe's green and bitter worm, a horrid toad-black beetroot alcohol, whisky, rum, and anisette, *prunelle*, a blushing peach brandy; and syrups: mint and lemon, angelica. . . . It was still early for customers and the Cod's wife was not standing in her usual place. The room smelled of roasting fish – surely the Cod's dinner. I walked over to the chimp's cage. Charlie Dee was fast asleep. His snoring made me think of walking on gravel at the bottom of a pool. Then my heart leapt, for I saw in the far corner of the room, smoke wheeling about his head, Toujours-Là. The dying sun sent a faint gleam through the nearly opaque glass and bathed his features in alarming shadows. Now I wonder what demon compelled me to navigate the dusk and to sit down at his table.

The old sailor was pouring out two fingers of Terminus brand absinthe. With as much ceremony as a trembling hand would allow, he cradled a lump of sugar in a pierced spoon, balanced this over his glass, and poured in water. When the absinthe swelled to the colour of sea water, Toujours-Là acknowledged me and greased his whistle.

The liquor in the Ghost was served in thick, hand-blown tumblers the like of which I've not seen since. They were very old and the Cod had inherited a seemingly endless quantity of them when, no longer fit for seafaring, he had bought the place, handed his wife the brass key, and gone upstairs to give himself over to toothache, piles, and melancholia. The Ghost's glass tumblers were so heavy, and the lip so sound and smooth, that they commanded love and respect. I'd heard of men throwing bottles in anger in that place, but no man had ever smashed a glass.

Toujours-Là licked his lips, cleared his throat, and said:

"I've travelled the world over and I've seen the Devil *everywhere*. But nowhere, Nini, nowhere, mind you, nowhere have I seen God." He sucked his teeth, took a drink, and twitched.

"Rose says –" I began.

"Don't believe the crap you hear!" he barked. "The universe and all its filthy planets were not created by God but by the Devil. Every morning the sun rises with an empty belly and at night she sinks bloated with blood. You've seen how the moon circles the world like a clean bone?" I nodded. "Like a skull licked clean of meat." he insisted.

"Like the face of the Ogress!" I whispered, fascinated by the gloomy colour of his words. Although I sensed that the mad steersman was about to ferry me across the starkest latitude of his imagining, already my own darkest waters were rushing out to meet his.

"War is brewing again, Nini; I feel it biting at my bones. They said Bismarck was a hound – *all* men are hounds! The Devil's hounds! And women are hornets. *When was the last time you saw your mother?*"

I was stunned. Toujours-Là, having momentarily emptied his gullet of bile, took up his pipe and for a time kept quiet. But I, at least within, was anything but quiet; my blood was in a turmoil. I tried to remember when I had seen her and could not. It was like trying to see a midnight path in a starless, moonless air. But then, unknown to me, the quicksand of my thoughts shifted, and I changed the subject.

"Tell me a story!" I breathed, curiously exalted as when once I'd leaned too close to a cage of vipers a tattered man was showing for a *centime* in the street. "Tell me another story; tell me, Toujours-Là," I rambled on as stiff in my chair as Pinnochio before he was made flesh, "tell me another one, about her – about the Ogress –"

Just then the Cod's wife came downstairs with a dish of baked tuna and pan-fried potatoes.

"So you're here, Nini!" She pecked at my cheek and striking a match lit a lamp. "Where's Totor?"

"I don't know – I'm out alone! Out exploring!"

"I'll bring you a lemonade," she said, "a hot lemonade with bitters. But no rum, Nini. Rose was in, mad as a cat – you're not supposed to be here, son."

"I'm big enough to know where I should be!" I said dramatically, and to prove it pulled off my wool cap and threw it down on the table – just one of the heroic gestures I'd stolen from Maximinole. When she had gone Toujours-Là said:

"The woman's always mothering me and wants me to eat. I tell her: '*This* is my meat!' " He held his glass to the light. "You want some supper?" The food looked good and I had been wandering since breakfast. He pulled the biggest folding knife I'd ever seen from his pocket. The tuna's flesh was so hot it hissed against the cold steel.

"I once loved baked tuna. But they say a man's a moulded river, little more than water. There's something to be said for an entirely liquid ballast." He knocked off another glass and with the ragged vocal cords of a rusty pail sang:

> "My woman's a bar lily
> with a heart of flaming whisky
> and the greenest eyes
> and the meanest ways, yes
> and the sweetest lies. . . ."

When the Cod's wife was back with my lemonade and saw

the empty dish pushed aside, she gave Toujours-Là a kiss. "Good boy," she said.

"Good boy!" he spat. "I'm old enough to be your grandpa – you silly cunt!"

"You watch your language in front of the child!" she bridled, hurt.

"I can hear anything!" I cried bravely. "My brain's solid copper!"

"If the old sonofabitch wasn't ready to croak," she explained, "I'd throw him out. Owes me plenty, too!" She slammed back upstairs.

I felt something pulling at my leg; it was Charlie Dee. He looked at me from under the table and grinned. I helped him up onto my lap where he immediately stuck his finger into my lemonade. Meanwhile Toujours-Là knocked his pipe out against the heel of his shoe. The ash tumbled to the floor. He took a curious beaded pouch from his pocket and scrounged around for a few fragrant shivers of tobacco. Then he refilled his pipe lovingly. I thought: One day, like Totor and Toujours-Là, I will carry a pipe. Hung before his face the mermaid sailed the air, and, like a steamship, smoked. She made the Ghost feel homey; she was, after all, a toy hearth. Toujours-Là poured himself another. This time he made a *panaché*; he mixed his absinthe with mint syrup and a spot of anisette.

"I was never a man," he began, secreting the bottles on the floor beside his chair, "to carry dung in a pocket to exorcize misfortune. . . . One morning I woke up *nowhere at all*.

"I was young, still wet behind the ears, in fact, Nini, barely twice your age; an apprentice ship's carpenter on his first time out, shipping with the Greenland Company and eager for adventure. We was after whales in Baffin Bay and we'd anchored off what's now known as Thule – the furthest point off the North coast of Greenland a big ship can sail. The night before, I'd sat myself down in the most peculiar bar you'd ever hope to see – it squatted like a bitch taking a leak. The beams and rafters was made of the ribs of whales, the sod walls was carpeted with seal fur and the one window was the stretched bladder of a walrus.

"Outside they was those boreal constellations hanging so glassy they set my teeth on edge; why, just looking at them was like chewing sand. There was something hideously timeless about the place, and the morning looked like evening and the other way 'round so you never knew what time it was or where you was, fore or aft, sleeping or waking. Hell, you had to think twice before sitting down else sit on your own face.

"The blue-eyed Eskimo who ran things had, by the smell of it, distilled the bile of seals; too many hours before I'd taken a swig and one – the orbs of my eyes had bled, two – my ear drums had burst, three – I couldn't feel my legs from the knees down, four – I began to feel warmer than I'd ever felt since relinquishing the womb (maybe warmer), five – I'd apparently begun to sing Offenbach, six – I was dancing on the table in my socks while my head orbited the room, and seven – I was out like a candle and under the table in the dimmest corner of a dark room, a room wherein everything was barely perceptible, lit by a couple of sputtering walrus-oil lamps.

"Despite the considerable rumpus I'd made in the infancy of the evening, my mates and the polar proprietor had forgotten all about me. When I woke up I found that my granddaddy's pocket-watch was gone, but I still had my pipe." He sucked on it thoughtfully, curing the cleft between the mermaid's breasts with a filthy nail. "I ran outta there like rats from a hull on fire, but the sea was as empty as an overturned coffin.

"I stood by the water, cursing – 'Devil take me!' I hollered, 'I'm marooned!' I repeat, I was *nowhere*, Nini; there was nothing in Thule, nothing but Eskimos and one crazy Dane trapper (and he's the one stole my watch for sure), and a couple of tumbledown sod wigwams, plus that damned cabaret tucked inside the ribcage of a leviathan, and the frozen heads of slaughtered reindeer marking the end of the street, their ears gnawed off by polar foxes which gave them an especial dismal appearance, *and above all ice* – ice, ice, ice – thousands of square feet of the stuff underfoot. I was standing on ice, Thule was anchored on ice – just thinking about it, even now, gives me vertigo. Water's one thing; ice another. I'd rather wed a witch than be marooned on ice!

" 'Devil take me!' I cried, 'I need a ship! Any ship!' In that beggarly light I looked with despair on a horizon larded with *ice*!

"And then, Nini, I see her. I see: Bel. She materialized like an uncorked genie in the middle of downtown Thule, halfway between a pyramid of frozen walrus guts and the public shithouse.

" 'Hello, sailor,' she mewed, 'you're wanting a ship and I have one. I'm always on the prowl for sailors,' she purred, and she gave me a wink.

" 'You a ship's captain?' I asked, flabbergasted. I'd never dreamed a woman ship's master, and the wench was beautiful – if peculiarly dressed in an obsolete velvet with sleeves like bellows. She was wearing lots of jewellery; I particularly admired the wide choker of pearls. I took one sniff of her skin and the scattered pieces of my fractured skull came together.

" 'If you is a captain,' I said, 'where's your ship?' After all, I'd peeled the horizon for the *Søren Kierkegaard* and seen nothing but the bung-hole of a whale. She laughed and her black eyes gazed towards the ocean.

" 'I'll be damned!' I said again, because I seen a ship, Nini, such as I'd never seen before, and thank Lucifer, never since!"

"What was she like?"

"A species of barquentine but bloated, writhing with shapes indeterminate, ugly and obsh . . . obscure. Despite her size she was somehow volatile . . . a hammered air . . . a . . . what's the word? Coagulum, yes, a coagulum of night, suspended between the sea and the sky like a cathedral on fire."

"A cathedral!"

"From stem to stern she was carved like some hermetic cabinet with all manner of occult ribaldry: naked witches straddling billy goats and lunatic carpenters wielding their privates like hammers. There was queens kicking the posteriors of valets and kings with the vish . . . the visages of maniacs copulating with mitred bears; and preaching foxes and farting preachers – in short, a thousand devils and devilish devices, an encyclopaedic chaos wreathed with the names of rebellious spirits: Lucifer, Beelzebuth, and Astaroth; and magical words such as ZAITUX and TROMADOR in a muddle of griffins – but all rendered with such foh! felicity that though she could have looked ridiculous, in fact, the monstrous vessel commanded – in her wild and gloomy way – respect. Especially her mammoth figurehead."

"Oh!"

"She appeared, Nini, wading knee-deep in the brine, which, with each passing instant, looked less like water and more like a filthy chowder. She confronted us full-on, a giantess of blackened madder, so wonderfully carved she must have been the work of sorcery. Her haggard beauty was worried by a century of high wind and salt. The throat was thrown back in silent laughter, the teeth as big as casks of rum, the feral nostrils flaring, the orbits of the eyes like planets, the tangled mane of hair blazing with the phosphorescent algae that gave the ship the semblance of burning. The cleft of her bosom was so deep it could have held the bodies of three men; her nipples were broad enough to straddle."

I laughed.

"Laugh, will you! Little sprat! Only *listen*! At those massive thighs, the spheral knees, the foam sputtered and died. Suddenly the sea was still. So much *dead water*, a gum, a pitch –"

"A co-agulum!"

"A clotted pitch! 'She suit you?' Bel asks. 'Her name's *Great Babylon*. And mine's Bel. Now let's drink to seal our contract.' I find myself standing in a richly appointed cabin on board, Bel proffering a brimming cup. As I drink, a story I heard long ago rattles in my head: *The woman was dressed in purple and scarlet trimmed with gold and gems and pearls: in her hand she held a golden cup filled to the brim with abomination. . . . On her forehead was inscribed a mysterious name: Great Babylon. . . . And I saw that she was drunk on blood.*"

"And was there blood in the cup?"

"No, boy, sweet wine. One taste and a whirlpool is spinning in my mind and before nodding I am sleeping. I awaken in the belly of the *Babylon* in a hammock next to twelve others, all empty. Sticking my head up the hatch I smell roasting and baking, and follow my nose to where Bel and her crew is feasting. I'm greeted with raised cups and pull up to a table set like an altar with all my favourite dishes: veal stuffed with prunes, and duckling with sauerkraut, and egg pudding swimming in caramel –"

"Rose makes that!"

"So I've heard. . . . We is a motley crew in our stained monkey jackets keeping company to a captain who looks more like a countess. Coopers, harpooners, blacksmiths, common sailors – sea-dogs all, and who, from what I gather, have all been saved from calamity: bedlam, suicide, starvation, shipwreck – even hanging for murder. Bel is like a mother to us, that fondant bosom heaving as she passes the platters.

"Then the cook staggers in with a flaming Alaska. He's the strangest character imaginable. Looks like a hyena trotting around on hind paws and swathed in an apron. I needs look twice to see a man; yet swear I hear claws clattering like meat forks on the deck.

" 'Tell these worthy tars tomorrow's menu,' beams Bel. 'A menu's like a lullaby,' she confides to me. 'I like my men to sleep.'

" 'We sleep a lot,' a deck-boy yawns. 'A-a-a-a.' He drops off then and there, his forehead in his pudding.

" 'Eggs Rosita!' the cook attacks the menu with a yelp. 'Eggs Rossini. Baron of lamb *à la byzantine*, Scarlet Beef, fried *animelles*, moussaka of mutton, a partridge *estouffade*, a salad *arlésienne*, braised salmon, pigs' trotters with mustard sauce, sea-bream served in melted butter, scallops Mornay, stuffed shoulder of veal, smothered –'

" 'Stop! Stop!' we all cry together as if afraid to die of too much happiness.

" 'I, ah . . . uh, eat when I, ah, sleep . . .' the deck-boy sighs, still sleeping. 'I sleep when I, e –'

" '*Cèpes*! Fruit *rissoles*, rhubarb pie, pudding *à l'anglaise*, jam omelette, Bourdaloue pears, soufflé Erzsebet, frangipani, Devil's food –' howls the cook. It comes to me that all my mates look like sucking pigs – their faces so round and plump and their colour so high.

" 'A Sauterne will be served with the Devil's food,' Bel flashes her teeth, 'and with the pigs' trotters, a Moselle. And now,' she breathes, 'our toddy before tucking in!' Bel smiles at me and winks. To tell the truth, I think this winking's vulgar for a captain; then again I suppose a captain can never be a *lady*.

"Bel, it is clear by her attributes and attitudes, has been around. She is no white lily, but more your scarlet poppy, and her petals, lovely as they is, is mussed. Sounding my thoughts she gives me a slow, sideways glance which causes my stomach to sink. But then she's handing me a fragrant cup. Inside I see a ring of imps cracking whips and leaping hoops of fire."

"Oh! Don't drink it, Toujours-Là!"

"It smells so pungent and delicious, I quaff it down and I'm sent flying into the familiar whirlpool to the sound of

trumpets and more prosaic the baaa baaa baaaing of a thoush –
thousand sheep. I awake the next morning feeling unstrung
and queer. But the smell of frying beefsteaks and fresh coffee
has me and my mates leaping to our feet.

"Each day at breakfast Bel gives us our orders: retracing
her chalk tetragrams (and the Devil knows their purpose), and
scraping the rust off these iron coffins she cherishes, their
insides fitted out with sharp nails, and swabbing down the
timbers of the ship, those huge, hot decks. But scrub with
bucketfuls of elbow grease and good, brown soap, still a
dreadful phosphorated mould is always growing back, coating
everything in a luciferous sheen. Yet there is never much else
to do as the *Great Babylon* sails herself, her canvas groaning
day and night in an unceasing wind. We is going somewhere
very fast, but in a haze so thick only Satan could say where. I
fear we'll hit ice, but Bel says she knows no finer helmsman
than the Infinite and His wind. I figure that the Infinite of
whom she speaks is no other than His Highness of Infinite
Hell. In the mist I sometimes think I see His furies knotting
the latitudes and longitudes that net the globe, tugging, and
twisting, and dredging for our souls.

"Since I am a carpenter, Bel has me repair the *Babylon's*
ancient witcheries – those lewd emblems worried by the salt
of time. Some of these – the griffins and the bears – is badly
worn about the rumps and muzzles as if in their static race
around the bulwarks they has been tearing one another to
pieces. Some is lost their noses, some their teeth, others is
featureless. Sculpture were never my line and the stuff the
Babylon is made of is dreadful dense. I wonder how, despite
the outlandish humidity, the wood is so hard and dry. An
unworldly fire consumes the ship from within.

"Nights I dream the *Babylon* is made of rotting flesh, and
fractured bones and tiger's breath and tar," Toujours-Là continued, pouring out another *panaché*, "but Bel likes me and
shows it by cuffing my ear in this kittenish way she has. Once,

young fool that I am, I grabs her and gives her a kiss. For this I get a scratch from my temple to my chin what don't heal for weeks. She is a demon, no doubt; keeps her pronged tail tucked beneath her petticoats.

"We all feel poorly. Some complains it is for lack of exsh . . . exsh . . . Oh! Hang it! Or blame it on the constant wind wish, dammit! DAMMIT! For a polar wind ish God-dammed hot *and getting hotter all the time!* I, for my part, blame it on my su . . . sup –"

"Supper!"

"Shhh! Suppurating cheek which ish badly inflamed, and a nasty rat bite I've got on the neck, which gets to hurting worse as the days pass. The others – why, they's bitten too; the *Great Babylon*, scrub and scour as we do, is infested with rats and it maddens us that if we hears them scuttling all the time, and all of us bit – *we never see a one of 'em!*

"THAT MONKEY STINKS!" he shouted then for no apparent reason. "THAT MONKEY STINKS TO HELL!" Startled, Charlie Dee tucked his head down under the table. "Speaking of in – fah! – *infested* – I can see his lice from here! SET HIM DOWN!"

"He's clean," I said. "The Cod's wife gives him a bubble bath each Saturday and rubs him down with lavender water. Totor told me. What happened then?"

"Time . . ." he said, shivering, "time is speeding by unstop-pable. Time's a broom bewitched, straddled by a hag. Have we been given the Devil's red shoes to dance our lives away? Are we eating the Devil's pudding?"

"We is!" I shouted, tremendously excited. "We is!"

"SHUT YOUR TRAP!" the sailor barked. "Each day when I awakes I try to think, but the pain in my head is too horren-dous, and the hunger in my belly has me stumbling with the other fools to that charmed table.

"STOP TOYING WITH THAT CRITTER, LAD!" he shouted savagely. "Set it back down on the floor or stick it in its cage. You want to hear the tale or fuss with animals?"

"But I *am* listening, Toujours-Là, I *am*! Charlie Dee's not doing anything. Please. And then? What happened then? It's the Ogress! I know it is she! Bel and the Ogress – one and the same!"

"Yeah," he said. Then, in a low snarl I did not like at all: "Yeah, Slyboots! I could tell you another story. . . ." He lifted his glass to his lips and delved for the last few drops of liquor with his tongue.

"Listen to me, boy," he hissed. "Listen at the chinks. Listen if you want to know what hides beneath the tides, the shhh . . . swiftly ebbing tides of air you breathe. Prick your ears, my suckling; I want to hear your ear-bones crack! Listen sharply! ARE YOU ALL EARS?"

This tirade ended when Toujours-Là was seized by a painful spasm. When he took up the story again, his voice, thick and rumbling, was hardly recognizable.

"We is all growing weaker. Despite all that sleep and fancy fare we look like starvelings. All my mates is ulcerated at the throat – the punctures are deep and ugly. Did I say we was thirteen at table? Thirteen counting Bel?"

"I don't recall, Toujours-Là."

"You recall! Little bugger! Heed me! I am dreaming. . . ." He waited. I was angry and did not ask about his dream. He looked at me intently and, only after a long pause, continued:

"I am dreaming about black widow spiders what eat their mates, you know. Mantises do it, too. In the act. Eat the male's head clean off *in the act*. You ever seen that, little bugger? Ever seen the Act?"

"Toujours-Là," I whispered, my head swarming, "I think I should go home. Rose –"

"THE STORY AIN'T OVER!" He reached down and plucked a bottle from the shadows. "I consider throwing myself into the sea, but Bel, always so good at leeching onto my thoughts says: 'These waters are swarming with sharks.' Now, if the thought of drowning is beginning to appeal to me, I have no desire to be eaten alive. It takes all the courage I have left to ask: 'What waters, ma'am? *Where are we?*'

" '*Where* is not your concern,' she says. 'I hired you as ship's carpenter, not as ship's philosopher. How dare you ask *where*? *There is no where*. Nor will there ever be.' Throwing back her gorgeous head and exposing her long, white throat bound in its pearl bandage, she roars with laughter. Outside the wind swells and echoes her hilarity.

"One morning I awake slick with sweat, a shrill shriek, possibly my own, tearing through my ears. I've been wrenched from a vivid nightmare of a winged and whiskered creature crouching heavy on my chest, its barbed proboscis boring into an artery, its thread-like tongue worming into my brain. The pain at my neck is esh . . . excruciating. Near mad, I see the others in a haze, sleeping still as Death, each one bleeding a thin, yellow blood at the neck. Despite my horror and my weakness, I know I must solve the riddle of Bel's floating *Babylon*."

"Did you? Did you, Toujours-Là?"

"No! Her griffins have kept their secrets, and if it was they what steered her, or Satan's own shadow – neither you nor I will ever know!" He circled his tumbler's rim with his thumb. "I penetrate to the heart of her; I explore the hull's baleful maze. So tortured by fear and pain, I have to stop each step to hold my aching head in both my hands and weep. I find nothing! Nothing in the main hold. Nothing in steerage. Nothing in the afterhold, or the captain's store. She carries no cargo but these empty iron coffins and I am sorely baffled that with no ballast in a gale, which by the second doubles in velocity, the *Babylon* doesn't rise into the air.

"I come at last to the galley – there is nothing there – not an onion, nor an apple pip; nothing but a sinking feeling and, Heaven help me, a mangy cur, scaled and patchy, outlandishly filthy and seemingly exuding a noxious green sss . . . smoke. He's sleeping in the centre of a chalk circle I've retraced myself.

He opens one rheumy eye and, curling back a purple lip, shows a set of teeth I know I have no use for. When I see his shadow rising on the wall, I leap for a ladder and, pushing through the scuttle, find myself looking up into my captain's cabin."

I must have squeezed the chimp too tightly in my arms then, for he squirmed and, pulling away from my embrace, sprawled across the table and knocked over the sailor's glass. Toujours-Là gave Charlie Dee a slap which sent him sliding to the floor. He stood whimpering and stealing angry looks from behind his fists. Stunned, I mopped up the absinthe with my handkerchief.

"I see," he continued, pouring out another, "I see – hanging from the rafters in the dim glow of that evil ch . . . chamber, hanging heavy and sodden from its feet, its wet muzzle glistening in the darkling air, *an abomination* – the creature of my dream. She is the offspring of a mantis and a bat, her teeth like prongs, her furry belly pendulous and swollen. Had she been a creature of the sea, no matter how hi . . . hi . . . hideous, I would not have been so afraid; it is the wedding of insect and mammal in the middle of the ocean what strikes me as particularly hidsh . . . hidsh . . . horrible. A bead of fresh blood ish hanging from her snout and this thing, this frenzy escaped from some lunatic's reverie is" – Toujours-Là hesitated and, squinting at me, I think gleefully – "*is wearing a pearl choker*. And the blood she is drooling, child, *is my own*." For emphasis, Toujours-Là jabbed at the air before my face with his pipe. Charlie Dee reached out and struck his thumb down its incandescent bowl. Grunting surprise and pain, he knocked the pipe to the floor where it shattered.

Toujours-Là leapt from his chair and swept the chimp up by the ankles. He raised him high and sent him fracturing, head first, against the wall. With a sickening thud, Charlie Dee collapsed in a heap, spitting blood.

Having scrambled to my feet, I fought for breath. Upstairs, the Cod lifted himself out of his tub.

"WHAT'S GOING ON?" he shouted. "WHAT'S GOING ON DOWN THERE?" The Cod's wife pushed him back into the suds and pounded downstairs. Charlie Dee lay knotted in spasms. With a trembling hand, Toujours-Là polished off his glass.

When the Cod's wife screamed, I ran. I ran as fast as I could away from Toujours-Là and the Ghost Port Bar. But the Ghost Port Bar and Toujours-Là have always followed me.

After the murder of Charlie Dee, Toujours-Là disappeared.

"Good rubbish," said Rose. "May he never be seen again!" Two slow days passed before I returned to the Ghost with Totor for the monkey's funeral.

CHAPTER

7

The chimp's cadaver lies on the polished surface of the bar flanked by glasses of rum. The Cod's wife hovers over it, her red eyes fortified with mascara. Her grief is genuine but, as is mine, abating. Ignoring the rum I reach for a waffle.

Upstairs the Cod lies liquefied with rage. He had no special affection for Charlie; it is his wife's infidelity which has submerged him in gall and vinegar. He believes the universe has signalled him out for contempt, and in the monkey's murder perceives the monotonous bane of cosmic mockery.

"I've been thinking, Nini," Totor takes me aside to discuss this man to man, "how being close relations to chimpanzees and other apes like gorillas and orangs, how all of us here – you, me, the Cod's wife, the Marquis – could be standing around in our fur and like baboons, sporting scarlet behinds, or – like other monkeys I've seen in pictures – elegant manes. While Charlie here could be stretched out in his skin as hairless as a nun's elbow. I've heard that old orangs are often bald, Nini, and that's what got me thinking."

"He was just a baby!" the Cod's wife laments, "not much more than four. Come all the way from the Congo, poor fellow, in a cage. It was Bottlenose gave him to me –"

"Bottlenose had a sixth sense," says Gilles, a man with bristling eyebrows and a moustache to match, "and a nose like a –"

"Diving rod!" cries his brother, Gillesbis. The twins carry

their bones in their pockets – that is to say, their dominoes – and as they finger these unceasingly, their conversation is punctuated by the sound of small, ivory bricks in collision.

"He could smell sardines in the air," says Gilles. "Said they smelled sweet and –"

"Stale!"

"O his dear little face!" the Cod's wife sighs, fiddling with Charlie's hem. "I always thought his face was like an upside-down ace of clubs." And because this confuses everyone, the Marquis pulls out his stub of turquoise pencil and makes a little drawing beside Charlie's feet so we see what the Cod's wife means:

"Bottlenose said: 'Sardines smell of –' "

"Beer!"

"Charlie smells of lavender," I cry. "He's dead but he smells like a garden!" The festiveness of the wake has given me wings. I only wish she'd dressed the corpse in trousers and not a human baby's baptismal gown.

"I'll tell you something else. Bottlenose could see where the fish was swimming, even in the –"

"Dark!"

"Said they left a –"

"Shining!"

"Why?" The Cod's wife dries her eyes with the back of her hand. "What made Toujours-Là behave so crazy?"

"Everybody goes crazy sooner or later," says Gilles. "Just look at –"

"*Bottlenose!*"

"Totor," I ask, "just who *is* this Bottlenose?"

"Well Bottlenose, Nini, was a treasure-seeker, and, I guess, a little cracked –"

"He had a nose for fishes," says Gilles, "and so he thought he had a nose for –"

"Riches!"

"Once Bottlenose shipped with a freighter to Africa –"

"Took a steamer up the Congo –"

"He was crazy for adventure –"

"Farted higher than his arse!"

"Bottlenose," Totor cuts in, "told about how every night on the river he was kept awake till dawn by the gibberish of river spirits. The more he listened, the more convinced he was they was talking about a treasure –"

"He had this obsession. Should have been smelling –"

"Fish!"

"Not the fumes of –"

"Fancy!"

"Hell, Nini, those regions are full of everything but the kitchen sink, and it is a sure thing what Bottlenose took for ghosts was the lovesick cries of crocodiles. Maybe he was hearing the bottom of his boat scraping the backs of fishes; I hear the Congo's got some prehistoric varieties with scales like soldered armour."

"Bottlenose listened and listened," says Gilles. "He thought he heard the spirits saying: *Tusks and pearls. . . . Tusks, tusks and pearls. . . .*"

"Weren't it skulls? Skulls and pearls?" asks Gillesbis. "He had this sixth sense, like Gilles says. Maybe he heard *something*."

"Aah. Bottlenose was always blowing his own trumpet," says Gilles. "Hearing things. Smelling things. Bottlenose and Jeanne d'Arc – both crazier than –"

"Bedbugs!"

"He was always a brooder –"

"Hatching castles in the sky!"

"He heard *Tusks!*" says Totor. "And sometimes he heard *Skulls*! And oftentimes he heard *Tons. Tons of pearls*. And *Scads. Scads of Tusks*. We are talking ivory, Nini. Worth its weight in gold!"

"He dreamed of a skull –"

"Filled to the brim –"

"With pearls!"

"So Bottlenose went cir –"

"Cum –"

"Ambulating!" says Gilles, "while we stay here, fishing. And not for compliments, neither!"

"No, Sir!"

"Me and my twin brother here, we ain't –"

"Dreamers!"

"We ain't poets!"

"We ain't pre –"

"Sumptuous!"

"We," the brothers say together, "is fishermen!"

"You're forgetting," says Totor, "just how *good* Bottlenose was. He's earned the right to a little wanderlust – he was the best man on the coast!"

"The first fish of the season was always his! 'See how the water's thick and oily,' he'd say. 'Here's our fish!' "

"And they was!"

"He'd point these things out to us –"

"The oily water –"

"How it would get all nubbly."

"How the puffins –"

"Was behaving."

"But when he got back from Africa –"

"He was always dreaming."

"And drinking with you know who –"

"Who we ain't mentioning his name."

"Toujours-Là," I whisper, thinking how somehow, sooner or later the old demon worms his way into the best stories.

"Shh! Yes! He's the one we ain't mentioning!"

"Now, one night," Totor continues, "Bottlenose had a dream as clear as that picture hanging in the frame." We all look with misgiving at a sepia photograph behind the bar of the Cod and his wife standing in front of the Ghost looking younger and deadly serious. "He sees the skull carved of ivory and the pearls. And all in a solid gold box deep in the mud of the banks of the river Congo."

"So he buys himself a sca . . . a scatch –"

"A diving suit –"

"With a helmet screwed to the top like a upsy-down fishy bowl –"

"He tries it on."

"He looks ree-diculous!"

"He sets off for La Rochelle the next morning –"

"Where there's a cargo bound for Banana –"

"Lashed to his folly like Odysseus –"

"To his mast!" Suddenly the Marquis is at the piano hammering the keys and the twin brothers, their eyebrows hopping, are singing in booming baritones:

> "And Bottlenose sailed for Banana
> with a skull full of pearls for a prize,
> but the treasures of our dreams, son,
> are the scales of butterflies.
>
> And he'll risk his life for a gold box
> that is swimming in his head;
> and the only skull he'll ever find
> is the one he'll find once he's dead."

"*Is* he dead?" I ask Totor. "Is Bottlenose dead?"

"Must be!" cries Gilles. "That diving suit was –"

"A scramble!"

"It was –"

"Asymmetrical!"

"We *can't* bury him in the cemetery," the Cod's wife breaks in, "though, dammit, I paid for the plot – hook, line, and sinker – and got the family members laid away there as it is. I explained all this to the curé. Said my mother won't mind sharing her patch of sod with Charlie Dee; quite the contrary. Grandpa neither. Well – they're much too far gone to mind *anything* –"

"And being in Heaven –" says Gilles.

"Feeling charitable," says Gillesbis.

"And if in Hell –"

"Too occupied –"

"Begging for mercy –"

"To care!"

"Every one of them loved animals. It's not as though he'd take up room. I said to the curé: 'He'll keep the baby company.' The curé said: 'Charlie's no Christian.' I said: 'Baptize him.' But he refused. So I said: 'Then bless him, damn you! You bless the ocean, you bless the fish; you can damn well bless Charlie Dee!'"

"*I'm* blessing him," says the Marquis, "*now!*" He dips his finger into his rum and solemnly sprinkles Charlie's phiz.

"If we had a little boat," I cry, inspired, "we could put him out to sea and let him float away like Tristram and Zoé! Like Rose told me –"

"Like Iseult." Totor corrects me.

"What Tristram loved!"

"The baby's cradle! Tina's tiny cradle!" The Cod's wife runs upstairs.

"What baby?" I ask.

"Hers – what died, son, years ago."

"Totor?"

"Yes?"

"Charlie Dee's wearing that baby's dress?"

"Most likely. That baby of hers wasn't around near long enough to grow into it. Say, Nini – you had a good idea there!" He gives my arm a squeeze. "See how pleased she is!" I look up to see the Cod's wife thumping downstairs with the cradle. It is a vulgar object, heavy and thick, and it looks more than anything like a dough-trough painted white. I see at once that the thing is too short; indeed, once the chimp is laid inside his feet stick out over the end. The Cod's wife solves this problem by draping Charlie's feet with a lace antimacassar.

"He looks like a fairy princess!" the Cod's wife says, rocking the cradle on the bar. It is not true. In his white half-shell, dressed in lace, Charlie looks more like a monkey than ever.

Because it is snowing, the Cod's wife covers Charlie's face with a clean linen napkin. We are six to pull on our jackets and stomp out into the sharp daylight; seven counting Charlie.

"WHERE ARE YOU GOING?" the Cod calls from upstairs. "WHAT'S GOING ON?" he booms, piteously. Everyone pretends not to hear him.

By the time we arrive at the breakwater we are dusted in snow.

"Like whiting dredged in flour –" Gilles begins.

"And on queue for frying!" cries Gillesbis. As the sea's steely pan swells beneath us, we stand together and watch the Marquis carry the cradle down the steep stone steps to the water.

"Say something first," the Cod's wife calls down to him. "Say a little prayer. Say . . . how does it go – *ashes* –"

My mind is wandering. I am thinking about how time for the men of the Ghost Port Bar is counted out in the sea's abundant loose change; how the seasons have these names: Sardine, *La Drague*, Skate, Mackerel, Sardine – and how December – too dangerous for these men's small boats – has no name. Charlie Dee is being launched on his last voyage some time after Sardine and before Dredging.

"Dew to dew," the Marquis says gently as he sets Charlie down upon the ocean's Great Way. "All things dissolve."

"All things are dew –" says Gilles.

"Charlie Dee, me and you," says Gillesbis.

The Cod's wife and I are weeping when he gives Charlie a push. Compressed in death, the chimp lies huddled in his white ferry, the antimacassar preceding him like an altar.

For several instants the bark glides forward, but then turning suddenly upon itself, it circles back, tips, and capsizes – projecting Charlie into the water. Charlie sinks like a loaf of lead. He sinks so swiftly we see nothing of him – not even a trail of whiteness. We watch as the crib's pale underside is carried out to sea.

CHAPTER

8

Feeling cheated and a little foolish, we tread back through the quickening snow to the Ghost. On the way I hear a hammer and catch a glimpse of sparks leaping beyond a blacksmith's window. As Totor and the others walk on, I stop to admire the mysteries of fire. The room is dark, the smith invisible. The ringing sparks strike my eyes and ears with the force of a full-blown hallucination. In that room fire is the embodiment of sound.

The cry of a fishwife pulls me back to the frosty reality of the street. Shaking the snow from my hair I set off to explore the city's ancient quarters, a secret itinerary traced out by cobblestones so humped they hinder walking. These regions embrace the Ghost and the Galaxy and, further on, a curious establishment of precarious solidity: the Snail and Shark, wedged between a sinister-looking bottling works, and an abandoned bindery. A handsome devil is painted in diluted colours directly on the wall. He holds a toddy in one hand, and a glass of black coffee in the other:

COFFEE BLACK AS SATAN
TODDY HOT AS HELL!

The devil faces a small square, and a fountain which plays by fits and starts. Worn by more than weather, a featureless figure surges from the foam like a frost-bitten finger. A trickle of water sputters in the dirty ice crusted at its feet.

When the season goes well this object is rewarded with the kisses of seamen's daughters, but once I saw a priest climb into the fountain with a whip. As he lacerated the statue, he held his skirts up with his teeth.

This square also boasts a junk shop with a receding roof of sparse slate tile. And if I never pay much attention to the clutter in the window, today, the day of Charlie's funeral, a handsome china monkey catches my eye. I stare at him, my face pressed to the glass, and he stares back at me. The pupils of his blue eyes are intensely black. His body is a pale yellow, he has a white belly, a butter-yellow beard, and a violet nose. He is sitting on a fanciful throne of violet-glazed rockery. He looks shiny and new, like an expensive piece of marzipan.

A seascape has been propped up behind him. In the ocean's depths the Heavens are reflected: the brightly burning spheres of the planets, the moon, the blazing stars. I look at the painting and wonder if Charlie's body must fall as far to reach the bottom of the sea as his soul must rise to reach the gates of Paradise. And I think that the monkey is intended for me; that we are intended for one another. What I feel for him is no less than passionate love. His face, animated by a gently mocking smile, seems to say:

"So! You've come at last! Can you do it? Do you dare?"

Apparently the room beyond the window is empty. Ignoring a scowling griffin with wings and talons spread above the door casing, I peer through the dusty glass. I see more paintings in heavy, varnished frames, barometers and bells, a thicket of oil lamps, parasols, and canes. Holding my breath, I push the doorlatch down slowly with my thumb.

I suppose there must be a bell strung to the door. I open it millimetre by millimetre until the space is just large enough for my face. Without thought, my heart leaping, my body follows my head – and I am standing in a low-ceilinged room, which smells of violet-scented tobacco; I am kneeling on *The Lives of the Saints and Martyrs*, I am reaching around the mysterious seascape, and I am seizing the monkey. And to the sound of my own violently drumming heart, running down the street as fast as those treacherous cobblestones and my own heavy clogs will allow – with my prize, cold as ice, tucked inside my jacket. But just as I pass the Snail and Shark, I am seized in turn by the scruff of the neck.

"*Thieving*, are you!" Toujours-Là whispers hoarsely. With his free hand he cruelly twists my nose. I try to pull away but he has me captured. "You're not going anywhere, Nini; I've been wanting to talk to you. Totor know you're out stealing? And Rose?"

"Not stealing," I mumble. "Just taking care of it."

"*Taking* it, you mean. I should take care of you! Bah! Nini – don't be so scared of me. I feel bad about Charlie Dee. Come on, son, the punch is on me. Sinners should look after one another."

I follow Toujours-Là inside the Snail and Shark. It's a far bigger place than the Ghost, and nearly empty. The rectangular room with a worn, wooden floor, once painted black, is heated by a grotesque kerosene stove. As its fierce heat hits my face a tear tumbles to my lips.

"Your victim," Toujours-Là hisses, pointing to a small, silver-haired man who – arms dangling at his sides, his cheek to the table – appears to be asleep. "Now, if he'd been awake, Nini, and sitting where *I'm* sitting. . . ." I turn my head and across the square, see the façade of the junk shop clearly. I laugh giddily.

"That's the stuff!" Toujours-Là broadly grins. "One must be light in crime: light as a feather."

"But it's *not* a crime, Toujours-Là!" I whisper. "Please! Don't talk so *loud*!"

"Have it your way, boy. That thing buttoned up in your jacket? You stick it down between your legs and take your jacket off. It's hot as Hell in here."

Slamming a door behind him the barkeep appears. The junk

dealer starts in his sleep and Toujours-Là shuffles over to the bar for two toddies, one weak on rum and strong on lemonade. I bed the monkey between my knees and cover him with my coat.

"I could give him back," I say when Toujours-Là returns.

"You *keep* him. Takers are keepers."

The toddies are served in pewter cups. I notice dented brass spitoons in every corner of the room.

"Witness to an extinguished race of fantastically powerful men," says Toujours-Là, "who drank toddies of liquid mercury, and who spat lead bullets." I sip my own brew feeling easier.

"What's that word – *extinguished*?"

"Out. Like candles. Means a race don't no longer exist. Pfft! They's why the fog's always so thick in this city. We is living among ghosts. They was once big and fearless, a race of monkey men – and that thing you stole is an effigy of their greatest king: Thingummy Ma'Hoot. Thingummy chewed bars of brass for breakfast!"

"But he looks so kind!"

"When you is as powerful as he was you can afford to be kind."

"Are you telling true?" I whisper. "Because he's not a monkey *man*, he's, as far as I can see, all monkey." Peeling back my coat I ask Toujours-Là to take a look.

"He's got two arms, two legs; he's sitting up like a man, he's got this majestic, professorial expression on his face. Thingummy is a monkey man, Nini, of the race of Ma'Hoot. I've no doubt about it."

"You won't tell?"

"I'm not telling. I've thieved in my time." I notice then that Toujours-Là is wearing an ancient, green coat, threadbare at the sleeves. If the coat is stolen property, I doubt the owner misses it.

"How's the Cod's wife?" he asks. "I did her an evil turn,"

he admits gloomily. "Times there's no way escaping my evil temper. It's alcohol makes me ferocious and queer. I've done worse than murder monkeys. Hell – I feel bad about Charlie Dee and intend to make up somehow. But *how*?" He tongues his gums thoughtfully.

"You should tell her you're sorry."

"Mmm – well, I'll do that – I'll get her another monkey. I'll have to *steal* it, though." He winks. "Well. It ain't tragedy. Her heart ain't broken. And if the Cod's wife's been kind to me, a woman's kindness is a two-edged knife."

"That's not true!" I cry, scandalized. "Other Mother's kind. She's good. She cares for me, she does, she –"

"Yes. Rose is kind. But then she's simple. You gotta admit she's simple. The simple can afford to be kind."

"She cares for me!" I insist. "And the Cod's wife cared for you!"

"Bah! She's just scared I'll talk to the Cod. About her goings on. I could tell you a thing or two about her goings on. The *goings on* of a woman is fearful, Nini. Worse than what a drunken fool can do to a chimpanzee. So tell me – I hear they was a veritable funeral. A wake –"

"Oh! Toujours-Là," I cry excited. "*Bottlenose!* You *knew* Bottlenose!"

"Folks was talking about Bottlenose at Charlie Dee's wake?"

"They was!"

"About how he went off and damned well disappeared?"

"Looking for treasure! They say he died."

"Last night I saw the ghost of Bottlenose," says Toujours-Là, and his eyes of a he-goat, wicked and wild, burn into mine igniting the candles of my mind. "I saw him as he'd always been: a drinker, a seaman, and a dreamer; his nose a beacon shining like the perpetual fah! flame at the altar of desire! The rest of his ghost was pale and trailed his head like the tail of a comet; he moved like a sleepwalker, slowly, with arms outstretched; his body was a smoke. His face was a spherical cloud, and his eyes was blind. The Dead, you see, live in obscurity. His tongue was black. The Dead eat dust, Nini, and mud.

"Old Bottlenose was as obsessed as ever, anxious, and dissatisfied. To tell the truth, I wouldn't have recognized him – Hell – I wouldn't have *seen* him, mist that he was, but for his nose, that blazing flag. If his shadow had abandoned him, his nose was still with him, more fat than thin, more long than short, more hot than cold, more red than white, more erectile than flaccid, more useful than most. This was the only nose I've ever known which could unlock doors; a regular shoehorn and once he'd caught a shark with it. There was a nick out the middle ever after that was handy for carrying the lantern back up the wine-cellar stairs. His nose was a shelf; he kept a pantry up there: a ham-bone, a plate, forks, and spoons; a breadboard it was; I've seen it pass the pickles and root out truffles, squirrels, foxes; why, once in Holland he stuck it up a hole in a dyke and saved that country from flood!"

"I've heard about it! But, Toujours-Là – it was a little boy that did it. Stuck in his finger –"

"Just goes to show how folks distort the truth. True, he was little then, his first trip out, a *mousse* – but it weren't his finger, it were his nose. He was born with it. A Caesarean – cut from the womb like a plum from a pie. A beautiful baby, white as snow, looking like the angel screwed to the top of a Pope's canopy. But the nose gave the toddler a diabolical aspect. His ma abandoned him on a convent's stoop; the sisters took to him at once – there was no end to their dallying with the babe. He ran off, a *mousse* at seven because the nuns was suffocating him with their attentions. Anyway, last night I recognized my old friend's proboscis at once.

" 'I'll find it now!' cries Bottlenose's ghost. 'I'm sure to find it now.' Even dead he dreams of treasure as he scales the shadows. But he's after something far more precious than before.

" 'The philosophical stone!' cries Bottlenose. 'Oh, there are celestial hierophants what will pay dearly for it! Once I find it I'll buy back my life, my precious, precious life!' Life *is* precious, Nini. . . . Why am I wasting mine away? I am wasting away. . . .' "

"What happened then, Toujours-Là? What did the ghost of Bottlenose say then?"

" 'I mus' find it and I will! I have all Eternity –'

" 'An' plenny of spirits to help you, too!' I said to the ghost, trying to be friendly although my teeth was chattering fearfully. Hell is far more populous than earth!"

"Why is one stone so precious, Toujours-Là?"

"This stone's a glass of wonders in which to see the past – perhaps the only thing that could entertain a celestial hierophant with an eternity on his hands to kill. *And why do I kill time?* I've got so damned little left!" He slams his fist down on the table.

"And then?"

" 'Alone!' cries Bottlenose. 'I'll find it alone! The Prince of Night can't give light to *all* the shades of Hell!' "

"What happened on the Congo," I asked. "Did your boat sink?"

" 'FEVER!' Bottlenose's voice was like a dead leaf swept along a gutter in the wind. 'Fever 'fore I had a chance to get my senses back, my bearings. I was misled. I listened to stories 'stead of following my nose. Had I followed it I'd be wallowing in gold coins now, 'stead of dew!' "

"What's gold smell like?" I asked, thinking to profit by the answer.

" 'Gold has the reek of lions on it, fulvous, and hot, and an atom of soot. Above all: gold smells of bile. But I'm off! I mus' be off! Give my best wishes for the New Year to the boys. Buy them all a drink in my name.' He pulled a coin from the air and here it is. Keep it, Nini; spirit money brings luck."

The coin looks like a bent brass washer. I put it to my nose. It smells of Toujours-Là's pocket. "Smells musty!"

"Been knocking about in some subterranean digs. Think of it, Nini! We're up here sitting on the crust enjoying life and just under our feet Bottlenose is plodding along day in and day out after his stone. Life is a twinkling and Death forever; down there when one shade meets another it says: *Remember? Remember the hot sun? A burning glass of rum?* And that reminds me. . . ." He pulls himself up from his chair and makes it slowly to the bar with his empty cup. I steal a look at the junk-store man. He looks the way the Cod's wife's goldfish look when their water needs changing.

"Toujours-Là," I ask once he is back, "you still not eating?"

"Not eating." He sucks on the brimming rim of his tumbler before sitting down. "I'm on my last legs, son, yet I haven't felt better 'n weeks. Yesterday I felt like shit and God knows I'll probably feel like shit tomorrow. But today I feel almost sprightly. It was watching you what done it!" He sits down laughing softly.

"How did Bottlenose *die*? Did he tell you *how*?"

"He did. Told me the entire story. How he'd chugged up the river Congo leaving direction to chance smells. How he inscribed his sensations in a little book. He was lonely, but then, who isn't? Strange birds shat in his boat and filled the air with shrieks. The water was so full of fish it was like cruising a *cotriade*.

"Then he began hearing curious rumours. The folks he met up with during brief encounters on the river bank all had stories about something fearfully bizarre further up river. Something they venerated, but at a distance – something downright magical. Bottlenose, always exalted anyway, got fixed on this. He figured it had something to do with the treasure he was seeking. So he took out a map and made calculations, thought so long and hard he got feverish. Every-where he saw clues, firefly arrows pointing out waterways in the dark. He'd get all steamed up over an unusual configura-tion of trees and when his rudder snared in weeds he decided it was time to leave the river and explore the land. Sure enough, a boy wearing nothing but a hummingbird's wishbone told him there was something strange and powerful not a day's walk into the bush. Bottlenose followed the boy to his village where he questioned the elders who all flocked around him wanting to rub his beak for luck. Bottlenose touched them too. Said their skins had a decidedly greenish hue and it came to him in a flash that they was the direct descendants of an amphibious race of mammals all as green as frogs. Too bad he didn't have time to develop his theory because –"

"CRABS!" comes a cry from the street, so loud it startles the junk-store man who bleets a little in his sleep. "Crabs! Crabs, crabs, CA-RABS!"

"– it just could mean that old Charles Darwin was wrong and mankind descended from –"

"CLAMS!" This time the cry comes from further away. "Clams! Clams, clams, CA-LAMS!"

"– salamanders. Anyhow, maybe these green-hued natives egged Bottlenose on, maybe not; maybe they *did* believe there was something mythic and powerful haunting the jungle. They said it never slept nor moved, but only stood its ground and stared; a silent Cyclops this were with a weird, inhuman aspect, and three-legged to boot, though some argued its third leg was an inordinately long penis. Yes – a powerful demon, bright-eyed and intent; the guardian of some terrific secret, some enchantment, some open sesame, some (Bottlenose was sure of it) –"

"Treasure!"

" 'A heathen statue, no doubt,' says Bottlenose, 'a hoodoo hocus-pokery. A totem pole tomfoolery. A quackery. In other words: just some humbug idol.' But if the rumour smacked of mumbo-jumbo, it smelled, Nini, of gold; Bottlenose's rocket glowed." Toujours-Là attempts to stand.

"At night it lead the way
Burning bright as day!

"Ah! But the jungle was thick! Treacherous! Bottlenose himself was growing fearful of the thing! What if there was a Cyclops crouching in the shadows waiting to grab him, and skewer him through and through and *through*, and roast him over a slow fire!"

"*Was* there a Cyclops?"

"Hold on! Bottlenose stumbles through a terrain like some demon's idea of a practical joke: vines like a hangman's nooses, and tar pits, and quicksand – not to mention crocodiles with tails rigid as saws. But Bottlenose walks on, though his eyes near pop from their sockets with fever. And then in a clearing, he sees it. Sees that brooding Cyclops with one tireless eye and outsize member."

"What does Bottlenose do!"

"He collapses, Nicolas, in a fit of mad laughter. He laughs so hard the parrots tumble from the tree-tops because what he sees is only an old camera perched on a tripod and bleeding rust! There's a wasp's nest stuck to one leg and a buzzard's turd crowning the top and the whole thing's tilting precarious. A skeleton lies beside it picked clean as a pin, dressed only in a grin, a pocket-watch and a locket. Bottlenose laughed the harder, weeping as he roared, to see that the skull greening in the grass weren't ivory but bone, the locket, gold plate; the pocket-watch, brass.

"That night he succumbed to jungle fever. Bottlenose died contemplating the photographer's stopped watch; now his own bones lie beside the other's. Who knows what stories *that* marriage will engender among superstitious folk! Say – tell me – can you see the clock up on the wall?"

"I can!"

"Then read the time. Is it near three?"

"It is! Ten to three!"

"And today is Sunday?"

"It is!"

"Ah. Then it is time."

"Time for what, Toujours-Là?"

"Time to take a plunge into the air. Time for a lesson in Natural History. Time to see. . . ." He pulls himself up from his chair and lays a worn coin down on the table.

We leave the Snail and Shark for the familiar maze of streets. The air, cold again, speaks clearly of a snowless night.

Toujours-Là ducks down an obscure alley, keeping his balance by leaning against the filthy wall. When he climbs a stone staircase, its iron railing torn away and veering blindly into space, I refuse to follow.

"Come!" he coaxes, "I'm going to show you Blue Beard's closet!"

"No! I don't *like* Blue Beard!"

"Shh! No reason to fear. Don't you want to see the fatal forest? Don't you want to see the dragon?"

"There's a forest up there? There can't be. You're making all this up!"

"Shh! You'll wake him!"

"Who?"

"The dragon!"

"There's a dragon up there? Truly?"

"Beautiful and terrible! Shh! Not a word, Nini, now; not a sound. He sleeps in a chamber of fa! fa! *fire*! You don't want to wake him!" I follow Toujours-Là down a dark corridor which smells of mice.

"Behind that door!" he whispers, squatting on the floor and pulling me down with him. A hole has been bored through the wood. Illuminated from behind, it shines in the shadows like a tiny star. Toujours-Là puts one eye to the hole and silently laughs. I am both frightened and devoured by curiosity.

"The castle of love," says Toujours-Là, "and its abysmal moat. Look!"

Is there a Devil in the room? Or has something devilish happened to my eye? I see a bare, papered room with windows veiled in tattered lace and blazing in the sun, a soiled crimson quilt spilled across the floor, a length of brass bed and in a turmoil of sheets – the Cod's wife naked on her knees and thrashing in a weird forest of arms and legs. Stunned, I blink, and look again. This time I recognize the twins – Gilles and Gillesbis – naked as seals. The Cod's wife is prized between them; one twin is holding her by her unbound hair and the other slaps her rump. The fur at the base of her belly is so black as to be almost blue.

Through a vortex of blood I hear sounds which must be coming from the walls, the floors, the incandescent window, from under the bed – but surely *not from them*. The sounds are not human. I am horror-struck, perplexed, unsure of what I have seen.

Moments later as we walk down the reeling street, Toujours-Là says by way of an explanation and perhaps to justify himself:

"The room's my own. It's the Cod's wife rents it out for me. Nights I sleep there, see; days it's hers." As I remain silent, he continues. "Now you know what women are, Nini. But you ain't seen the worst. Blue Beard's closet is *fathomless*."

CHAPTER
9

Back home Rose is in her kitchen. The house smells of freshly baked custard pie. I carry Thingummy Ma'Hoot up to my room and lay him down beneath my pillow beside Erzulie. I imagine they form a couple.

In the kitchen the pie, speckled brown and yellow like an egg, steams in the centre of the table. Afraid Rose will see the afternoon reflected in my eyes, I screw them shut to receive her kiss.

"You're as white as a sheet!" says Rose. "Why are you making faces? Where's Totor?"

"We just gave Charlie Dee a nautical funeral –"

"Heaven forbid!" She sets a slice of pie down before me with a clatter.

"Read me the recipe for *abricots à la Condé*, Nini, and don't muzzle your food." She slams the great red cookbook beside my dish and, collapsing in her own chair at the table's end, begins to peel potatoes. "I've not seen much of you!" she scolds. "You're always out galoshing and I wonder where to? Not that I'm asking, mind you, though I've a right to know." And, knocking the earth off a potato: "Where've you been?"

"Out. . . ." I pretend to take an interest in the cookbook.

"Out *and* about, I'd say!"

"*Poach the apricots in vanilla syrup,*" I begin, "*but first slice them in two.*"

"Obviously! How ladle-headed does Escoffier think I am?"

"*Don't let them cook too long –*"

"They're already cooked; cooked and bottled just as they should be. Each time I use this book I think he takes me for a goose!"

"But he doesn't know you," I mumble with my mouth full of crust. I sit back, chewing dreamily. The pieces of the puzzling world slide closer into place.

"It's good to be home!"

"Home is where the heart is," says Rose. "Cut yourself another slice."

"*Drain them and dress a border of sweet vanilla-flavoured rice pudding, well-thickened over the fire with two egg yolks, 150 grams rice, and a good piece of butter.*"

"Madame Pierre bought some of that comical vanilla," says Rose, "and used it. She shouldn't have. They all ate it, the entire family. Might as well feed pins to pigs. I'd rather die than cook with comicals."

"What happened?"

"Nothing *yet*. What's next?"

"*The rice should be soft, yet stiff enough to support the fruit –*"

" 'Time bombs in the kitchen,' I said to her."

"*Set the fruit on the pudding. Decorate with candied cherries and angelica cut to look like leaves. See picture page 446.* Look, Other Mother! It looks like a basket of fruit!"

"Do you think Aristotle will like it?"

"The Marquis will *love* it!"

"There should be little cakes to go with it. Find me a recipe for little cakes."

"Maybe you are an *Ogress*, Other Mother!"

"What an idea!"

"Fattening me up so you can eat me after! Other Mother . . . was my mother . . . someone *nice*?" Rose, her apron ferrying potato peel, bustles to the trash box and then to the stove.

"What did you say, Nini? Oh, handle it! I've burned my

finger on the kettle again!" She works the pump handle furiously and a cascade of icy water bounces from her finger into the stone sink, submerging my question in a vortex of foam.

Dinner is over. The ruins of the pudding are pushed aside; nothing is left of the hen but her bones, and the little cakes are reduced to atoms. Behind the etched glass of the dining-room doors Other Mother prepares coffee. Outside, a snow, like tufted fish, is falling.

The Marquis prods the fire. Totor, his pipe between his teeth, tells how a half-century ago an entire ship's crew vaporized in a mysterious fog in the port of Amsterdam:

"Nothing remained but the captain's gold teeth. The girls – no longer girls – still talk about it. The riddle weren't never solved, nor ever will be!"

"All things pass," says the Marquis, "all things, that is, but mystery. . . . Look at the battlements in the fire, Nini!"

"Looks inhabited from here!" cries Totor. "See that devil there, swinging from a donjon! Whoops! There he goes –"

"And there goes the donjon!" A tower of embers totters and collapses.

Outside the snow falls faster. As when sitting out on the breakwater watching the ocean slide past, I pretend it is I who is moving, tonight the entire house is rising into the sky, and with it, secreted beneath my pillow, Thingummy Ma'Hoot.

Thingummy's silence, his teasing smile, force me to heed my own nagging doubts and to indulge my curiosity. Within the week I am breathlessly searching in Rose's top dresser drawer where I know she keeps her secrets and, therefore, mine. Tucked away in a faded blue envelope among letters from Totor dating from his seafaring days, and their wedding menu printed in gold and stained with wine and gravy, I find a photograph of a couple sitting together in a rowboat. Without being told, I know that these are my parents. In my father's face I recognize my own, and the oval of my mother's face has been carefully rubbed out with sandpaper.

Father is an intense-looking young man in this thirties, dark, with eyes sparked by an endearing glint of good humour. His smile, as he gazes upon my mother, is affectionate. He looks like a man with a full life ahead of him, yet in two years he will be dead.

Family connections have not yet been clearly defined. It is not until the spring I am told, having for the first time asked, that father was Totor's nephew. This much clarified I return to the blue envelope.

The afternoon is mine. I have time to ponder the question Thingummy – sitting on the dresser, a small, stolid oracle – has provoked. Why has Rose removed my mother's face when she could have cut the photograph in two?

I study my mother's figure for clues. Her slender neck and arms are visible and her hand reaching for the water which – I see it now – is not there. This is, in fact, a studio photograph, and the mossy banks and weeping willows painted canvas. The lake itself is an unrolled sheet of paper.

Looking up from the fictitious lake, wrinkled, a seam ill-concealed, I continue to investigate the country of my mother's faceless body. She is strangely swollen, *as if*, Thingummy prods, *she is with child*. My breath catches: *I am that child*.

This is why Rose has kept the entire picture: *I am there*. The thought that I might have been severed from my father to sail unborn in a half-boat, in a fictive landscape across a phantom lake fills me with such dread I forbid Thingummy Ma'Hoot to ask further questions. As that familiar screen of palpable shadow unfolds once again in my mind, I put away the photograph and, holding Thingummy to my aching solar plexus, go back to my room.

Yet my investigations continue, if obliquely. I lead what Doctor Kaiserstiege later calls "a double life." Life with Totor, Rose, and the Marquis (for he has become a member of the family). He has convinced Rose to write a cookbook "peppered," says Rose, "with the antidotes he's picked up the world round such as those cremated Easter chickens and, for example, fastidious information about the vanilla trade, and even a recipe for fisherman's soup – the one they boil up on deck with sea water." And my other life – those hours of ice and fire that I spend in the company of Toujours-Là.

I can't stay away from the Snail and Shark, at least not for long. Saturday after school I find myself transported as if by magic to the fountain and contemplating that gaily painted Devil from the street. Despite the risks, I often bring Thing-ummy Ma'Hoot. He is the tangible ghost of Charlie; he has power. The fact that I have stolen him, necessitating secrecy, assures that power. And because Toujours-Là knows, he is powerful too, magical, a man of keys. Keys to the past, to the Land of the Dead, to the mystery of parents departed – but not at rest. His knowledge of the story behind all stories is the tantalizing prize he holds up in the half-light again and again and always just beyond my reach.

CHAPTER
10

In April the canneries are humming with activity and the horse-drawn trucks packed with cans thunder down the streets to the port. In this season which smells of street-side *fritures*, fish guts and boiling oil, I find Toujours-Là pacing the fountain square anxiously with a large sack. With each step his filthy toes slide out from the gaping ends of his clogs, and in the sunlight his odd, green coat looks like it might shine in the dark. The sack emits eerie, muffled sounds. He hands it to me.

"You take this," he says, agitated, "to the Cod's wife. You tell her it's the damned best I can do."

"A monkey!" He shakes his head. I take the sack from him gingerly. "What's in there?" For all I know he's caught a snake.

"I thinksh," he says, "some sort of a parrot; an exotic speshies of some short. Shit!" He pisses against the basin of the fountain.

"GOD DAMN YOUR KNOB!" Startled, we both look up to see a crone craning from a window just above us. "THAT'S SAINT PETER!"

Stunned, Toujours-Là shuffles backwards and collides into me.

"She still there?"

"She is."

"The hag's unmanned me." He jiggles his penis morosely. I

94

follow him into the empty street. "Listen. You take the sack over there. I'd do it myself but I don't feel so good. I feel like shit, Nini. I've felt like shit before but thish ish exsh-sheptional."

I loosen the knot at the top of the sack and take a peek inside. I see one angry eye and hear a demonic chugging.

"It's a *turkey*, Toujours-Là!"

"So thash wash it is."

"WHAT'S GOING ON, YOU TWO?" the creature screams. "WHAT ARE YOU DEVILS HIDING IN THERE?"

"KEEP YOUR NOSE TO YOUR OWN ARSE-HOLE!" Toujours-Là shouts back, furious. She eclipses. "Beat it, Nini, The bird's been purloined. Hell! Makes me mad being cheated like thish! I should have known better than to deal with alcoholicsh. The man told me 'twas an exotic speshies. I see now he was a sh . . . a swindler."

"How's that?"

"This were a legitimate commercial enterprise. A swap, fair and square. 'Cept he were crooked."

"But you've got nothing to swap, Toujours-Là!"

"Sure! You forget, Nini. *I got the act.* I swapped a look in the hole for the bird! But the bugger promised a parrot! Well, if she can't mother it she can stick an onion –"

"I'm not taking it, Toujours-Là. You're the one owes her an apology. Not me."

"I thought I could count on you. If I can't count on you, Nini, who the Hell *can* I count on? But hurry up! Goddammit! It's soiling up the sack. What if it suffocates?"

"Maybe it could be plucked," I offer, "before you give it to her. Because she's not going to want it for a pet. It's got a nasty look, Toujours-Là."

"I'm not plucking it! Are you crazy?" Leaving the sack in the middle of the street, he turns and weaves his way slowly back to the Snail and Shark. I run after him.

"I'm not doing it!" We are still arguing on the stoop when

a four-horse factory truck loaded down with two tons of canned sardines comes wheeling down the street with a tremendous, unstoppable, clamorous shudder. Toujours-Là pulls me by the sleeve into the Snail and Shark.

"Another one will be here any minute," he says, "an' there won't be an atom left of the bird. Let ush be philo-shopical. I say: GOOD RIDDASH. Did I tell you about the time, Nini, Bottlenose went to sea with a bellows?"

That night Rose came up with "an extremely delegant recipe for fish soup made dreamy and anxious by the addition of roe, garlic, and egg yolks pounded together with a porcelain pestle and wedded with heavy cream." The Marquis was the first to taste it and suggest additional pepper – after which Totor proclaimed the soup perfect. This soup contained brill, sole, spiny lobster, turbot, crabs and "a shy visitation of clams." She served it with little diamonds of fried toast topped with roe poached in butter. For dessert she made a lemon mousse, "because after supper the fish should be only a memory of the mind."

After supper I slipped upstairs and took the photograph from Rose's drawer. I squinted, trying to imagine my mother's face. Then, instead of putting the picture back, I took it to my room and laid it under my pillow along with Erzulie and Thingummy Ma'Hoot.

I returned to the Snail and Shark on Sunday morning. It was as deserted as ever. The dealer in antiques was there fast asleep, and at the bar a blighted woman pleaded with the snarling green shadows in her glass. Toujours-Là – the greater archon of that diminishing hierarchy – sat, as was his habit, brooding beside a bottle. I walked over to his table and with an anxious heart lay the mutilated photograph before his eyes.

He did not move. I was aware of the woman's soft bleating, the sleeping man's shallow breathing. I looked across the room into an immense mirror which hung at a weird angle; the vast rectangular floor and everything on it seemed to be sliding into unchartered space.

"Toujours-Là!" The old sailor twitched and, wiping the spittle from his chin with his wrist, appeared to fix on the picture with intensity. For a few slippery instants I feared he contemplated only the muddy well of his own thoughts. "Tell me!" I insisted. "Tell me what you know!"

"I knows plenny, nenny, *Né*-ni, Ni-Ni . . . *plenny of thingsh*, yeth, shit! SHIT!" he barked, pulling out a chair and nearly falling from his own with the effort. "You shit here, Nico-lath."

"Please. . . ." An eeling knot threatened to choke the flame which darted in my mind. I had to keep that flame burning. I pushed the photograph closer. It felt like a thin slice of ice. He picked it up. I saw his hands were ruined with age, shot nerves, and grime.

"Ni-na, na-na . . ." he sang inanely under his breath and it seemed an unforgivable blasphemy, no matter how terrible the truth, for the foul-smelling soaker to be pawing that precious artefact, the only trace that my parents and I were once a family. I was sorely tempted to snatch the picture away and run back to Rose's kitchen. I thought I had not really been home for months; I had been haunting an underworld. I asked myself at what moment I had fallen; for ever since the theft of the china monkey I thought of myself as *fallen* – a favourite word of Other Mother's. The Cod's wife was a fallen woman; undoubtedly, so was my mother. But the more I thought about it, the further back that feeling of falling seemed to reach, even preceding the night I saw the face of the Ogress in the moon.

That Sunday morning in the Snail and Shark, the droning of the drunken woman in the shadows and the sound of the sailor's humming in my ears, I knew that the underworld had always been with me. Toujours-Là's stories had only rendered it palpable. Exhaled from every pore of my body, my own natal inferno had swollen into a sort of all-encompassing fog. Somehow I knew that only the truth could cause that fog to lift.

"Wash hap . . . hap to her *faish*?"

"Rose, I guess . . . must have –"

"Better not look into the faish of Lilish!"

"She was called Lily?"

"Odille."

I took up the name *Odille* and turned it over and over in my mind, as I had so often picked a pebble from the beach and sucked on it to give it back its colour.

"Odille," he continued, "like odi-oush." I held my breath. "Like *Ogresh!*" He sat back triumphantly. Then he rubbed the empty place where her face had been with a filthy finger. He left a dark smudge. "There wash even a song about her. About them all. Whilst you wash tucked away in Rose's little spun sugar nest they wash singing about Odille in the sh-streets! Odille an' your papa and Thomas. Thomas – Odille's lover." I bit my lip and tasted blood. "I'm telling you all thish because when you ask questions you're old enough for ashes." I nodded, but the flame in my mind was giving off an oily smoke and threatened to choke itself, and Toujours-Là looked more like a corpse animated by necromancy than a man. Yet I wanted to know everything.

"A song? About Odille?" Toujours-Là began to hum and when he thought he had found the tune he sang in a weedy voice:

> "O the Devil iza woman
> She's the worl' beneath her heel
> an' she kicks it hard

like a spinnin' wheel.
Her eyes is midnight
her heart is steel
an' her name is Odille.

Odille put on her silk shoes
Wit' the pretty heel;
she took up her kitchen knife –"
"A knife?" I clutched his arm.
"Juz in the song. Ac-shually she din' have a knife. Twash
Thomas choked –" He began to hum: "Too dee, tee dee, te-
deum.

"O Thomash, foolish Thomash
O tell me what you've done –

"Tee dee, too dee-ah! Confound it, Nini. I can't recall the
thing. 'Cept the end goes sumpin –" He cleared his throat and
spat:

"An' now they is no 'ore.
Jus three corpses . . . three corpses on the shore!"

From the far end of the room the woman joined in boozily:
"Three horses on the floor –"
"Hey! Wun minute!" Toujours-Là cried. "Before the end it
goes: 'They was waiting on the beash wish stish!'"
"Beash? Wish? Stish?"
"Stishks! Stikshs! They wa-as waiting on the beash, see!
They *killed* Odille. And Thomash too!"
"Who?"
"Ev'rybody. Hiding they wash. On the beash. Behind the
sea wall. With stishks!" I attempted to decipher this. "Odille
wa' a witch. A booful witsh. An' he . . . an' he –"
"Who! He? My father?"

"He waza foo' – never knew wa wash going on. Innocent he wash aza new hashed hen. His head somewheres in the clows . . . he lived on the moon, notta man for Odille."

"It's not true! They drowned in a *accident*! Rose says –" My teeth were chattering.

"You know is shrew, Nicolath! What have I told you? Rose lies. Sweetenin' you up wiz jam an' bung-hole Bible stories knowing all along they ish a worm in your apple, son!"

"I –"

"What have I tol' you? The worl' ish evil, evil beyond the telling." A hint of tenderness crept into his voice and it only added to my feeling of despair.

"My mother –"

"They drowned her! Yesh! I wash there! *Watchin'*. Couldna stopped them, Nini, had I tried. They wash feroshioush! Odille and Thomash – they'd been seen, see, out on the water. Old Cod seen it all in his –"

"Bi-knuckles?" I whispered the word I'd learned from Rose.

"Sure. Seen how Thomash strangled your papa, how he choked him before throwin' him into the sea." Toujours-Là put his two gnarled hands about his neck and squeezed, sticking out his tongue and making me cry out in terror. "An' you sittin' there like a little clod o' clay, a little frozen seedling, bug-eyed, your mouth wide open juz like now!" He made another hideous face.

"Odille – she picked you up and held you tight. She wash shouting – the Cod could see that. And Thomash wash shouting, too. But the Devil knows what they wa' shouting about. *You* could tell me if you recalled; but you was too little. Couldn't talk after. Scared shitless, poor little bugger."

It was all true. That day out on the water I had awakened to an immense absence.

"They wash a crowd down at the beash waiting for them. The wimmen swarmed about Odille . . . held to her like flies.

An' they pulled her down. She fought like a fury but they wash too many. Thomash wash harder to kill; he wa' big aza bear. Big bones, big, broad back. Your papa's body was never found."

I was weeping. I tasted blood, I tasted salt. I loved, I hated Toujours-Là. Gagging on the words, I managed to ask: "Why? Why did she let him kill my father?"

"Odille loved Thomash."

Arm in arm, light and darkness dance upon the water.

CHAPTER

II

The first Sunday of May, the Marquis, Rose, Totor, and I took the train inland to the riverside village of Paradis-sur-Loire, famous for its thermal station and an inn: A la Recherche du Paradis Terrestre. We left home early with a hot water bottle's supply of black coffee wrapped snugly in a kitchen towel, and an outsize brioche. We ate our breakfast on our knees in the train as I counted station stops out loud and wondered about the origins of their curious names: La Folie, Ste Verge, Moisi. Rose had stories to tell and the unassuming stations, tidy and scruffy together as all things relating to railway landscapes, took on rich and variegated lives. Here an epileptic five year old had seen the Virgin Mary singing in an apple tree; here a notary had assassinated his entire family with a red-hot poker; here a monolith had toppled over and crushed a notorious thief; and here a man might see the face of his beloved blinking at the bottom of a well. Aristide said:

"You know how in fairy-tales a man sees his future lover reflected in his dreams? He carries her image like a precious jewel in his heart; he battles dragons and confronts entire armies, he survives imprisonment and humiliation at the hands of his enemies – and all this because he has *seen her face*. When at last they meet – and he must be man enough to recognize her even if she is caked in mud and wearing the skin of a donkey, or sleeping in a coffin of glass – the world comes sighing to a halt. Love tumbles into the arid orbits of his life like a meteor."

"And have you a sweetheart, Aristotle?" asked Rose.

"We met under curious circumstances," he said. "She was wearing the skin of a donkey and I wasn't man enough to recognize her until it was too late."

Before the railroad, the way had been traced by *colporteurs*, men dealing in ready-made clothes and household stuff: pails, frying pans, and brooms; cheeses and walnut oil; coal and wine. As we flew along, flanked by flowering almond trees and heaps of coal, I saw – there where the railway ran parallel to the ancient road – a gypsy caravan and, further on, a knife and scissor sharpener straining above a well-travelled carrier tricycle.

We also hugged the river much of the way; the broad, vigorous Loire rushing seaward as we sped inland past goat pastures and thickets and hamlets all unfolding beneath a perfectly cloudless sky. The distance covered was not very great, but with the many station stops the sun was high overhead when we reached our destination. The only thing to spoil our pleasure was the hot water bottle which, Rose realized with a wail, she'd "have to trot about all day!" Gallantly, Totor took it from her, the Marquis from Totor, and I from the Marquis.

In high spirits we turned down a dirt road worried by spring rains and the wheels of carriages. I felt the stiff ridges crumble under my holiday shoes. We now saw the spa's famous cupola shining silver beyond the trees and caught a glimpse of three graceful tiers of balconies. Designed by a famous architect, from afar the thermal station's Grand Hotel looked like a cabin-cruiser. It was all freshly painted and glistened white in the golden weather. When I was to see it again it would be very changed, the façade hidden by creepers, the great roof in disrepair, the grounds a tangle of roots and thorny briars.

We walked on, and in a few minutes came to Paradis. We took to the village at once – the tile roofs the colour of toast, the pale-green, weather-worn shutters and the soft, flour-white stone of the façades stained purple by the iron hooks which held the zinc gutter-pipes in place. Here and there in little niches, saints and virgins mutely offered their protection. Rose, acquainted with their histories of hardships, and to Totor's exasperation, greeted them cordially and expressed concern for their well-being.

As we crossed the village square we saw a brass band setting up in the kiosk and the proprietors of rival cafés lugging chairs and tables about beneath the new leaves of the linden trees in preparation for the afternoon's entertainment. Somewhere nearby men were playing *quilles*. We could hear the sharp sound the splintered spheres made as they struck the wooden bodies of the pins.

A la Recherche du Paradis Terrestre stood at the end of a shady street. At its back, gardens overlooked a grassy slope which in turn overlooked the water. The inn was a humble affair, but lovely, with narcissi at every window, potted laurel at the entrance, and three cunningly pruned pear trees scaling the façade. The stone structure was completely concealed by blossoms and breathing a vapour of scallions browning in butter.

In a corner of the courtyard bottles were drying, necks down in a bored plank, which bridged the backs of two chairs. This homey touch and the kitchen smells provoked Rose's whole-hearted approval. So too the menu, which, pinned in a box very like those street altars, included a pâté of crayfish and an omelette made with the sweet, spring buds of salsify.

How had the Marquis discovered such a place? We learned that he had worked for a time on a river barge delivering coal and lime to the village. He had seen the restaurant in this season and had vowed to return. I realize only now that he must have spent what small savings he had on that lunch.

The inn was run by two sisters. One paid the bills, scolded the waitresses, and charmed the clients; the other instructed the gardener, nagged the kitchen help, and cooked. She caught a glimpse of us from her kitchen window and, intuiting in Rose a kindred spirit, she called out:

"Say! Madame! Come see the trout 'fore they're cooked. Still kicking in the tub! I'm preparing them with hazelnuts."

Rose eagerly rushed past a pail of doomed crayfish and was swallowed head and body by the kitchen.

After a brief look at the garden, Totor, the Marquis, and I sat at our table in the sun and admired a menu written in an obsessive hand with purple ink scented of violets. I said:

"This menu reminds me of Charlie Dee." But I could not say why. The near-summer air wafted in through the open windows, and, if I noticed that the serving girl – dressed in crisp, new cotton and not much more than twelve – was very pretty, I was even more captivated by a sideboard, sumptuous with sweets. Grown under glass, the first strawberries glowed in dishes of porcelain beside a pitcher of cream. An immense tart of last winter's apples wept caramel. There was a pyramid of pears in brandy, and thin, fluted glasses of *sabayon*. Nothing rare here, no priceless, imported pineapples, but only seasonal things expressing plenty with art and love. I would have trouble deciding; fortunately, I would have plenty of time to choose.

Despite all that came after, I still remember that luncheon, the narcissi, the open windows, Totor and Rose holding hands under the table, the Marquis transforming the table-top into an impromptu theatre where dramas were acted out by butter shells and fish forks. I recall a spoonful of pepper transformed into a storm-cloud which threatened a painted Chinaman who, as the dish revolved, slipped under the cover of a napkin.

". . . And he heard the hail!" said the Marquis, tapping his plate with his fingernail. "And he said, 'How good it is to be in bed on such a night.'"

Totor told us about Atlantis, a hidden continent of Kings, so rich the streets glitter with gold nuggets; an enchanted land inhabited by creatures not animal nor human, but with the charms of each. Like centaurs, like sirens, like –

"La Vouivre!"

"Yes, Nini. Fish with the faces of women, their eyes pools of fire."

"Their voices melodious," said the Marquis.

"I should love to see Atlantis!" I exclaimed. "To see what no one has ever seen!"

"Once there were so few of us," said Aristide, "there were unseen places the whole world-wide!"

"Are there such places still?" I asked.

"The tops of some mountains, maybe," said Totor.

"The fundaments of troubical jungles," said Rose.

"And Bottlenose!" I exclaimed. "Perhaps he –"

"Just give me a hearth," said Rose, "a comfortable chair and a good, sharp knife for peeling potatoes –"

"For slitting throats!" I teased.

"Nicolas! Don't start that up again! He's got it into his head I'm some sort of *aggression* –"

"Ogress!"

"Rose – an ogress!" Totor roared with laughter.

"I'd rather voyage to the Holy Land with books," said Rose, to my relief – for all at once this talk of Ogresses had brought to mind Toujours-Là's recent revelations. "No buggage, no fevers, no accidents, no unsightly natives or customs like eating locusts, *pah*! No risk of capturing malaria or elephant-toes or losing one's way –"

"Yes, but think of it!" I insisted shrilly. "To see what no one has seen!"

"To see the fountains of Neptune!" The Marquis mussed my hair.

"Why Neptune?" asked Rose. "Nini! Quiet down. Are you feverish?"

"Because it is so far away," the Marquis explained. "So far it can't even be seen with a telescope."

"It would be lonely," Rose persisted. "Nini's ears are red." She caressed my forehead.

"Maybe not!" said Aristide. "That's what they said about the bottom of the sea: too cold for company. Too dark. And the pressure of the water like twenty locomotives pulling a full load of iron! But when they looked they found charming animals: diaphanous and beautiful –"

"Like lace!" said Totor.

"I bet the animals of Neptune are like that!" I was tremendously excited. "Di-aphanous, like the Marquis says, and charming!"

"But what do they eat?" Rose asked. "How can they possibly digest?"

"Perhaps they don't," said Aristide. Rose shuddered. "Everything digests!" she said.

Our trouts arrived as gilded as kings with parsley ruffs, and sliced lemons for crowns. The potatoes were new and they were not any bigger than walnuts. Rose was very animated; she had two precious recipes anchored between her breasts – one for the *sabayon* and one for crayfish *à la Turc*. And the cook had told her a dreadful story:

"Oh, far too dreadful to repeat. And I wouldn't want to ruin your lovely lunches! But a scandal, I assures you. Why, it's set me all aflutter. I hardly taste the pâté – and no, I can't let you in on it, well, maybe later. . . . To tell the truth my heart feels like a hen on a hot griddle!"

Just then I heard someone behind me say:

"I've blue feet!" Impatient with Rose's coy mysteries, I turned and tried to get a look at the man who was talking, but all I could see was the back of his head.

"I can't figure it out," the stranger said. "You'd think it was –"

"In pieces!" Rose threw her arms up in the air.

"A sort of –"

"Dead body!"

"Inside too! All the organs: BLUE! You should have seen me in a mirror! You would have said –"

"Her corpse!" Rose whispered.

"They stuck in so many needles, my arse was red!"

"You put a bucket down that well," said Rose, "it came up red!"

"Blue!"

"And they still don't know who did it!" Rose quivered with excitement.

As we ate, a burly grandfather clock kept track of the time ringing six times, at every hour and half-hour. I noticed that the mantel was decorated with a few porcelain figures, and thought of Toujours-Là and the demonic crockery he had once described. I thought of his turkey in the sack, and longed to tell the story.

"Is it true," I asked instead, "that Bottlenose went to sea with a bellows?"

"Well, yes, it is true," said Totor. "Who's been telling you stories about Bottlenose, Nini?" I lied and said I thought it was Gillesbis.

"Bottlenose had this theory about the wind. He said that everything is only 'agitated air' and he figured that if he could make his own wind, he could have an influence upon the world, people's moods, for example, not to mention the weather. I recall he said human speech, like clouds or a bad mood were just so much stagnant wind about the head. He believed that with a simple kitchen bellows he could navigate the ocean, dissipate fog and send storms chasing in the opposite direction. He used his bellows *sympathetically*, said there was an affinity between water and air. It was all quite complicated, Nini, but what it boiled down to was this: Out on sea it's dangerous to sneeze; sailors in animated conversation can – by the power of their own vociferations – change their boat's direction or what's worse – call up a thunderstorm. Or conjure up a school of fish. An ill-fated *langoustier* off the coast of Corsica was cursed by a continuous drizzle, trailed by a small, black cloud, simply because its captain – a heavy smoker – was cursed with a chronic cough. He used his bellows, see, with circumspection. He said in mild weather a lady's fan would do, or even a paper envelope."

"And did he go to the Congo with his bellows?"

"For sure, Nini! A red leather bellows embossed with curious designs of his own invention – he had it made up special for the trip."

"What nonsense!" cried Rose. "And pagan!"

"What was, uh, *embossed*, as you said?"

"Little fellows, all in a circle, with their pants down, making air."

I could tell that the man with the blue feet was listening to Totor. In fact, the entire room was quiet.

"Couldn't you!" Rose whispered sharply. "Couldn't you *for once*, Victor, converse *conveniently* at table! And in a fanciful restaurant, too!"

The Marquis handed her a tiny flower he made with a piece of cigarette paper, and under his breath he sang:

> "And Bottlenose sailed with a bellows
>   to the other side of the sea,
>   to the very edge of the world

where the crocodiles roam free.
'What use this thing you carry?'
the King of Banana asked.
'Sire, with this dia-bolical blast-bag
I make wind! Fore and aft!'
Thus I have no top, nor bottom
and when I make free
I navigate sweet Heaven –
a whirligig – that's me!
Forgive me, Sire, this madness
for it is but my faith –
and the object called a "bellows"
my fellow, god, and wife!' "

"I don't make head or tail out of it!" Rose wailed, precipitating a fit of merry laughter all about the room. But the exquisite *sabayon* soothed her, and after one spoonful she was mollified and forgave Totor and the Marquis their incomprehensible levity.

"*Their* ears must be buzzing!" she said congenially. She was referring to the angels. "They've only ears for sin," she explained, "and don't trouble themselves with the rest. Thank heaven one forgets that they are there, or one wouldn't talk at all!"

"What else do you know about Bottlenose?" I asked, smothering strawberries in cream.

Aristide said: "Bottlenose had this theory about friction causing heat, and how you could boil an egg if you could only manage to rub it fast enough between the palms of the hands without breaking it."

"Remember," said Totor, "when we pilfered all those eggs from the Cod's pantry?"

"Broke every damned one!"

"And that other theory – that if you threw the egg fast enough –"

"The friction of the air would boil it! Sure! I remember!"

"Oh!" I sighed. "I wish I had known Bottlenose!"

"Victor," Rose whispered, "just how many eggs did you take?"

"About twelve dozen."

"*Twelve!*"

"Stole eggs and saved lives. Every single one was bad. Smelled worse than the Devil's a –"

"VICTOR!"

"Ashpan – the Devil's *ashpan*, Rosie."

After lunch we stepped out into the swilling sunlight. As Rose and Totor sat nodding on the grass beneath a willow, the Marquis and I explored the river beaches. Rose had unpinned her hair and from the distance looked girlish, her legs stretched out before her. She had kicked off her shoes.

There were boats to let and I looked at them with longing. The Marquis proposed we cross the river. As he paid the man, I chose a turquoise boat the colour of that stub of pencil with which he liked to draw on table-tops. The prow was worn and the paint peeling, But Aristide claimed she was sound enough, unpretentious, and companionable. Her oars were nearly new. Her name was *La Puce d'Eau* (the water-flea) and this also suited us.

We left the bank in an orgy of birdsong.

"What a joy," Aristide beamed, "to be in a boat for pleasure and not to have to think of fish!"

But it was impossible not to. The water was riotous with startled fish, mating fish, rampageous, irrepressible fish. There were plenty of bugs in the water, too: water scorpions, water-fleas, boat flies with red faces, and oval beetles bright as lockets. It was good beyond words to be out on that living water with the Marquis. I closed my eyes and caught a distant smoke, the scent of woodlands, of wild roses, and decomposing wood.

We had reached the far side. Aristide churned mud and suddenly the water spawned a milky swarm of infant eels.

"All things pass," Rose liked to say after dinner or at a season's end. But that afternoon has never passed. I carry it in my heart, intact. I recall the sky's shimmer above the distant hills, the zithers and reeds of an eternal afternoon. Something precious caught, life-like, in amber. I recall each instant with a witching clarity; each instant is etched in my mind with a far-seeing chemistry. Even now, I smell the nutmeg of Aristide's skin and see his beautiful hands glisten on the oars. Even now, old and alone, I glide under a vault of leaves. The day endures, quickens, kindles and bursts into flame.

We rode out into a silent space. There was a hush as if the world had ceased to spin. When Aristide pulled up the oars we heard one starred bittern's ghostly cry.

"Make quiet play!" I begged. He looked confused. "Make those pictures . . . from nothing. It's like magic, Marquis – that *quiet play*. . . ."

"So that's how you call it! A clever enough name for *mes bêtises*." Reaching out, he pulled a phantom bird from the air, caressed it, and put it into a fictive pocket. The air was blooming, hatching birds like small fireworks or flowers. He coaxed them up his sleeves and down the neck of his shirt. When he was inhabited by birds, when one dozen, two dozen were scrabbling under his clothes so that he scratched and wriggled and I howled with laughter, he unbuttoned an invisible shirt and removed an invisible cap and prodded an invisible pocket, and the air was crazy with flapping wings. But one black swan with a neck as sinuous as Aristide's own arm did not fly away. Instead it dove in a fluid arc from his lap into the water.

I leaned over the side of the boat to look after it and cried out because I saw a face. I saw – by some trick of mind and light and water – *her* face, the face of La Vouivre, bubbles threading her hair like rain. My heart spilled into the sweet commotion of her eyes, and visited with a sacred clarity: *I saw my mother's face.* When a fish like a glyph of hammered silver darted from her lips I knew hunger and its capture; I knew seizure. And I fell for her; with a sound in my ears like a quantity of sand sliding down a very deep well, I dropped after her into the shivering water. I did not surface – although I knew how to swim – but gave myself to the green goddess of drowning freely, penetrated by a numbing sweetness. I was sucked in by a treacherous current; when the Marquis dove for me I was already gone.

When Aristide rose for air the world was chiming with frogs. A pair of dragonflies see-sawed in all their startling brilliancy above the boat. He dove again as I, lungs bloated with icy water, pulled up an inky mud with my dangling hands. It seemed I navigated forever. I was the prisoner of that dream I was dreaming when, no bigger than a fish, I swam Odille's salty womb beneath her darkly brooding heart.

The Marquis dove again. He explored the bottom of the river until La Vouivre claimed him as she had claimed me. He fought her, and when he thought that he would die she released him. Rising, he devoured the air.

Not far away he found me floating among the wands of reeds. He carried me to the beach and scraped the mud from my mouth; he forced the water from my lungs until he had me breathing. He rowed me back to the inn and carried me to the kitchen where I was stretched out on a long table, undressed, and rubbed dry. As the Marquis massaged my feet and Totor my hands, Rose stood by, shrieking, until the cook, returning with blankets, had the presence of mind to slap her.

I continued to dream. . . . *Looking up I saw the clouds, red against a yellow sky, tearing past with a hissing sound. Somewhere beyond the sky I heard Rose cry:*

"Drowned! Drowned dead like his murdered papa!"

Followed by a clap of thunder. . . . I had come to a city. It was evening and the streets were deserted. Turning a sharp corner I came to the house where I had spent my infancy. The house was a mill and its wheel churned a dark water. I saw Odille standing in her kitchen beside a deep well. She dropped in a bucket and brought up my father's head.

And still I dreamed: It seemed I had been floating for weeks in deep water among the soft bodies of jellyfish and the purple fans of plants. For an instant I thought I saw Aristide and Marquis pulsing past, but when I looked again he proved to be a sea-horse no bigger than my thumb. Somewhere beyond the sun I heard Rose say: "Water plays tricks."

I was drifting through the site of some catastrophe. The swell was ragged with a quantity of splintered wood and pieces of broken furniture. Barnacles had riddled beams and rafters with worming holes. A fiery multitude of starfish sunned themselves on a floating door. With a shock I recognized the door to my father's house.

And then I was inside the house, exploring the empty rooms. An ape who smelled of sour milk and onions suddenly grabbed me by the hair and pushed me up a ladder. A trapdoor slammed shut beneath me. I rubbed my eyes and in the blue flicker of a gas ring attempted to see. I made out a vast attic as cluttered and filthy as a knot in time. A baboon in a turban which made him look fragile as if his head had been recently fractured, sat humped over a table. He was up to his knees in sheaves of soiled photographs and with a piece of sandpaper tied to a spoon carefully rubbed the faces off all of them. A callused forefinger proved he had been at it for years. There was a box of bent spoons, the sandpaper worn, on the floor.

"You are quite pale and hairless," he said to me, although he had not once lifted his eyes. "You look sensible, however. That's consolation." He smiled sadly, as if this little speech was intended for a joke. He pointed to a stool and handed me a spoon.

We worked steadily for several hours. The photographs to be

altered were numberless. They crested in the pooled shadows of the room until they toppled over. "I'm seventy next Sunday," he confided. "A ripe old age for a monkey, you'll agree. I'm glad you are here," he added, patting me on the head with a leathery hand. "It's lonely in the attic, despite the bat. Lot's of company down there," he pointed to the floor, "but not our kind, eh? Infernal, eh? Eh?" Indeed, I heard shouting and music rising from under us like a filthy smoke flooding the room.

"There are bars in the city," he moaned, "and barmaids. There they are and here am I." He wiped away a tear with his fist. "I wasn't born a monkey," he explained.

From time to time the bat flew in from the dark recesses of the attic to help us. His technique differed from ours; he used no spoon but scraped the faces from the pictures with a razor-sharp fingernail about five inches long. The faces lifted from the paper like stiff little circles of tarnished metal. The baboon swept these up with his hand and polished them on his sleeve until they shone like freshly minted coins. He pocketed them and promised to buy me whatever I wanted. I said I wanted to go home. With a groan he bent over the table and, reaching for my face, gave my cheek a squeeze. Then he pulled a cold dish of lentils out from somewhere under the table and handed it to me. I told him I wasn't hungry. A fly struggled weakly in the gravy.

"Better in the gravy than walking around on your head." He smiled companionably. When I did not return his smile he explained it was a favourite saying among apes.

"The insects here all have very cold feet." This was the first time the bat had spoken. The baboon retrieved the dish and put it back under the table.

"Better a cold supper," he said, "with a live fly in it, than a hot supper with a dead rat in it."

"Give me a sweet roll anytime," said the bat, "with plenty of butter." Seeing me perk up he set me straight at once.

"There are no rolls nor any butter to be had in all the land for miles around. There's even a song about it."

"I'd give my all for a roll –" sang the baboon.

"In the hay!" sang the bat.

"I wasn't always," said the baboon, "this old."

There were books to be erased as well, page after page of finely calligraphed script and even maps. We erased the names of cities and bodies of water and roads and railways.

"Preparing for apoplexy!" cried the ape.

"Apocalypse!" the baboon corrected him.

"Our work was indescribably tedious and depressing. I thought that if I could only find Odille's face or my father's name written down somewhere, I could put a stop to all this. But the faces I erased were all unrecognizable and were – for the most part – the faces of baboons. As if he had been reading my thoughts, the bat then pulled a wallet from his pocket and, opening it up, pointed proudly to a picture of his family. They were all hanging upside-down.

"Enough!" the baboon said then, sweeping a pile of maps to the floor. "Have you ever played ape-chess? Ah!" he beamed. "It's the oldest game in the world." Once again he groped about in the shadows until he had found what he was looking for – a stained, dog-eared box of miscellaneous pieces. "It's like regular chess," he explained, "but not quite. And as I've not the proper pieces, neither, I've made up these you see! They are all of my own invention. This one, for example, is the Macocoscome. A most powerful piece. But having only spools and thimbles I've pasted on – although now it's torn – this star. The piece corresponds to the Queen. Ah! You don't play regular chess either! All the better!" he cried, undaunted. "You'll have nothing to unlearn and all to learn! For as I was saying, the Macocoscome corresponds to the Queen, but not quite. The bat and I refer to her affectionately as the Great Apess."

My head throbbed as he described her many moves and the treachery of a pawn made of a thimble and wearing a battered cone of red paper. To my relief a bell rang and, looking frightened and sheepish, the baboon thrust the game behind him. In his haste the Great Apess fell to the floor and was lost.

"She's fallen down the hole!" The bat offered to appease him, "Like everything does, you know, sooner or later."

"I don't see any hole," I said, getting down on my hands and knees.

"It's too black to see!" said the bat.

"It's so black," said the baboon.

"It eats every last part –"

"And particle –"

"Of light!"

"Why it's so carniverous –" the baboon continued.

"It's ridiculous!" The bat took off looping among the attic's invisible rafters.

"There's lots of stuff down here!" I cried. "Lots of cans of fish, and what's this?" Scrambling to my feet, I dangled a little gear on a string in front of the baboon's nose.

"It's the Galaxy!" he cried, snatching it away. "A most curious piece! I thought you were lost, dearest!" He gave the thing a kiss. "But here you are, you rascal! He covers the board in a twinkling of an eye!" he confided in a whisper. "Wreaking havoc! Even the Apess Herself –"

"I want to go home now!" I shouted.

"You can't!" said the bat from somewhere deep in that dismal room.

"Your home is wrecked," said the baboon. "Didn't you see it –"

"Poor nitwit!"

"– floating out to sea?"

PART
II

CHAPTER

12

A doctor was brought in from the thermal station. Doctor Venus Kaiserstiege was young, brilliant, and Viennese. She was also the world's only Freudian hydropothist. She had worked for several years under the guidance of Freud at the Psychoanalytical Institute in Vienna. When she left Austria for the spa at Paradis sur Loire, she continued to correspond with her former teacher. "The theoretical wars must cease," she admonished him. "Psychoanalysis will flourish only if its practice is based on mutual appreciation and the acceptance of many diverse, therapeutic methods. Dogmatism is poisoning your dream-child."

Some said that Doctor Kaiserstiege was a heretic, a mad-woman, and a quack, but she was accomplished and devoted to her patients with a rare tenderness.

From the kitchen of A la Recherche du Paradis Terrestre I was taken in an ambulance to the doctor's blue-tiled infirmary – Totor, Rose, and Aristide crowded in together beside me. Years later Doctor Kaiserstiege said that she had known at once the Marquis and I would somehow fill her life, which was true. But we filled her life only with our absence. . . .

As the Marquis carried me inside, Doctor Kaiserstiege showing him the way, Totor and Rose following behind, no one stopped to admire the hallway friezes so new the air smelled as much of linseed oil as it did of sulphur – cranes, ibises, and herons raising their wings and mating in a tri-continental landscape fused with all the careless licence of dreams.

For Totor, the smell of sulphur attested to the spa's authenticity, and was the proof of Pluto's complicity. It alone was enough to convince him that we had entered a supernatural place. Not that the spa was haunted; here the ghosts one met were always one's own.

It was the season of sardine and the Marquis had no choice but to return that very evening to the sea. Rose and Totor stayed behind. Silently they walked through the station's luxurious and extensive gardens without seeing them, or sat stunned like marble figures beside the marble fountains of the entrance oblivious to the Venetian-Viennese architecture and the perambulations of an international bourgeoisie and *petite noblesse* suffering from minor *maux*. In later years a Japanese dwarf wrapped from head to foot in a towel was all Rose remembered of her month spent in weeping at the spa. When they realized that they could do nothing to alter my condition, they returned to the city deeply grieved. Doctor Kaiserstiege knew that they were poor and, before they left, assured them that she did not expect to be paid. "Coma has long been my especial fascination," she explained. "Very little is known about it, you see." And she promised to write to them each week, to inform them of my progress, if any, and to describe her own procedures.

Shortly after Totor and Rose arrived back home they received a letter:

Life is a state of ceaseless restoration. The wound heals, the broken wing mends, the branch, burned by frost, sprouts new leaves. I am convinced Nini's sleep is a restorative sleep. However, he has been deeply perturbed by the shock of drowning. He is in the hands of a mysterious preserving power; he clings to sleep as a castaway clings to a raft. He must be coaxed or prodded into consciousness.

And the following week:

Nicolas has now been examined by members of the National Neurological Institute. They have approved my procedures, although they are experimental. Such cases are exceedingly rare and there is no habitual therapy.

All his senses are continually solicited. He is massaged and bathed twice a day. The waters here are very rich in minerals: magnesium, iron, calcium, sulphur. . . . He is given things to smell: roses, onions, ammonia, patchouli; particles of pepper and nutmeg are placed on his tongue. I've brought my own gramophone – I've some rare records of Chinese opera and monkey cries from the Amazons, but it is Strauss's Die Fledermaus *and* Tales from the Vienna Woods, *which appeal to him the most. His little face wrinkles in indignation should I wind up Beethoven! Throughout the day a nurse strikes a triangle near his ear, or rings a large bell. He dislikes the triangle and the bell as much as he dislikes Beethoven.*

These procedures are not as "magical" as they sound. More and more frequently the smooth surface of sleep is agitated, the stagnation of those deep waters disturbed, those muddy tides sparked with light. At times his face is infused with happiness; often he appears to grieve.

Appears to grieve – and this brings me to something we must all consider. I fear Nini's mind has been disturbed by more than water. In agitated dreams he calls out for his father. You told me that he is an orphan. May I ask how and when his parents died? You must realize that I am not asking out of idle curiosity. This is a delicate case. I should hate to commit an error when Nini "surfaces" as I believe he will.

Several weeks passed before Rose answered:

Error is sometimes preferable to the truth. His parents both died violently. Ignomously. It is best to leave sleeping dogs lie.

The doctor asked:

What do you mean by ignoramously? Perhaps you mean igno-miniously? Sleeping dogs may awaken and bite. To hide the truth is like trying to hide a burning candle under a haystack. [She was pleased with this and certain she had found the right formula for Rose.] *I assure you, I need to know all the influences which may have disturbed the dynamic action of his mind.*

And when this letter remained unanswered:

Please tell me about his parents. I could be wrong, but I feel it is fear which keeps him so stubbornly sleeping. And you, Rose, what do you fear? Please tell me the truth. You see – I believe knowledge is sacred. A sacred right. And that not knowing is always worse than knowing. The known can be faced; it can be circumscribed. Whereas the unknown is like a ghost. It haunts us, but remains formless. It cannot be seized.

But Rose refused to answer. When she wrote again it was to complain of Totor's own silence – for since my drowning he had refused to speak – and to ask what I was being fed. She approved of broths and herbal teas and eggnogs, but not of bells and triangles. She ignored the doctor's questions and redoubled her prayers. The doctor persisted:

Sickness is not a devil to be fought with prayers. Nini's mind is not inhabited by demons, but perhaps with painful memories. There is a theory to which I wholeheartedly comply: that a shock can lead to the denial of memory – a kind of willed blindness, which can lead to all sorts of nervous disorders. I see Nini struggle daily with that which appears to be a desire for and a fear of consciousness. In other words it is possible that he is afraid of waking up.

All this was lost on Rose who, I know now, if not incapable of understanding K's request, was unwilling to. To have understood, to have answered truthfully, would have meant admitting her own guilt, her own complicity.

To justify herself, Rose spoke to the curé. "It's just I'm not convinced," she said, "that the woman is reliable. What I mean is, she being a doctoress, sees men, well, *peeled*. Not even married and she knows buckets from pokers!" The curé shared Rose's distrust of female doctors. When Rose finally did answer K, she wrote:

Nini's parents drowned in a boating accident. Nini was a mere infant, just over two. He never knew what happened.

Doctor Kaiserstiege knew this was not the truth but the "preferable error." And if this is the preferable error, she thought, how much more traumatic is the truth? Whatever it is, she decided, he knows. And like the piece of apple caught in Snow White's throat, this knowledge will not go down!

The Marquis returned to the spa one Sunday in early August. He found K depressed – I was not responding to treatment as well as she hoped and her other patients were inhabited by an irresistible lassitude which lectures, surprise galas, and picnics could not dissipate. K was visited with the terrible certitude that her patients were at the spa not so much to mend their bodies as to kill time. It horrified her to think that what had been conceived as an island of love and light was nothing more than a genteel amusement park. She wondered if the same sedimentation was also taking place on the outside.

"They are all so stupendously blasé," she confided to the Marquis. "My little universe of water and quiet pale beside the jubilant, bombastic promise of war. When the dreadful news arrives it will be received with enthusiasm. What is to become of us if we embrace Evil as eagerly as we embrace entertainment?"

They were walking down an avenue of stunted palms. Turning onto a barely perceptible path they came to an over-grown corner encircled with boxwood hedges and busy with insects: scarabs, mantises, and crickets.

"This," she explained to him, "is a theatre intended for those inclined to solitary entertainments." And she kissed him. As she described it to me years and years later, they kissed beneath "the crazy-quilt canopy of trees and the world smelled not of sulphur but of chlorophyll and crushed leaves, clover and shelled shrimp." Knowing nothing of love, I wondered: Why shrimp? but was too shy to ask her to explain.

"My beloved acrobat," she said, "my merman of the air. Even now he animates my life. He was the only man I ever loved, and if he reappeared right now, walking up the path on his hands – I would ignite to be consumed utterly by happiness. You see, he gave me ecstasy; I had never known ecstasy. Oh, Nicolas! All these years I too have dreamed. . . ."

War was declared at the end of summer. Doctor Kaiser-stiege's patients packed their wicker trunks in a fever and cleared out.

At the station, a train festooned with flags and flowers churned past, choked with soldiers heading north. And, as K described it: "apparently thrilled to death. They were cheered as if they were on their way to a tournament, yet they were soon to find themselves up against all the unsoundable torture of obstinate matter. How gladly civilians and soldiers alike traded serenity for vertigo! Someone cried: 'We'll celebrate victory at Christmas!' Everyone imagined something fleet and coloured and noble. But Christmas came and went and the New Year, too. War was no longer the heady tumult of confronting armies out upon the open field; it was maddening stagnation in mud mazes and tunnels of smoke. The enemy had built a wall as impenetrable as the face of God. The price of a summer's diversion was our innocence and a stiff five thousand corpses a day."

Aristide Marquis was drafted that winter.

In the weeks and months following the declaration of war, the Neurological Institute sent K many unusual patients. Although their comportment varied tremendously, they were, as was I, all *sleepers*. The strangest case of all (if K were here she would hasten to say that her patients were "not *cases*! But people, people, *people*, Nicolas, in all their glorious singularity!") was that of the lovers – two tawny adolescents who stood mouth to mouth for decades in the ballroom empty of everything but forty-four slowly oxidizing mirrors. Year after year they stood in their own vapour, their skin as incandescent as the knives of druids. I believe they must have haunted all our dreams; I know they haunted mine. Somehow I saw them eternally burning on the outer edges of my mind. The smell of smoke which still permeates the spa – stronger, even, than the stench of sulphur – is not the odour of war but of skin kindled and rekindled with unconsummated desire.

And there was the cobbler. Although fast asleep, and often seized with tics – or what was more troublesome, the desire to bite – he continued to make shoes. If the materials at hand were not of the best quality he would go into a fit of depression so that K had to spend a fortune on suede and fine leather. As his production was phenomenal, and as he lost all interest in the shoes once they were made, all up and down the Loire Valley the impoverished children of wartime France, fatherless and dressed in stinking rags, wore the boots and slippers of fairyland: fox-brown, grass-green, blood-red.

These things K told me, stately and a little stiff, dressed in her silk shirt and linen suit of out-dated style, regal, self-composed, and tiny in a worn garden chair. She was close to eighty when I awoke to meet her, the only woman with whom it can be said I shared my life – such as it was. Or we walked, she wheeling me at the beginning, in the ruins of her ideal domain. In a breathy, brittle voice she told me all that had transpired since the day I had plunged into the dark waters of my own reflection. K despaired: the paths were overgrown with weeds and the fountains gutted with leaves. As I recall, I told her I thought her garden was a paradise.

"But Nicolas," she said, "Paradise never existed, nor ever shall. I fear your old friend Toujours-Là was right in his mad way; righter than the Marquis, though, God knows, I prefer *his* way. I have always known that Paradise is an impossibility. More impossible even than meeting up with a unicorn, or reading an opera written by a whale. This said: I have always behaved *as if it were possible*. And the only thing worth fighting for."

Of her many sleepers I was the sole survivor. I hasten to add that she was as unresponsible for those lost lives as she was for the burning of her own books. As she wheeled me about her ruined gardens of enchantment, the story of the world as it happened while I slept, unfolded.

As I have said, at the outbreak of the First World War, K lost all her regular patients and received only those the Neurological Institute sent her. The lovers, the cobbler, and I were joined by the eelman who, when not rooted in inertia, undulated like an eel, and a painter who rendered pictures of emblematic animals in the air with an imaginary brush. I see us as the inmates of an insane zoo, standing frozen in ridiculous postures, speaking in unintelligible tongues, shamelessly passing wind, communing with moonbeams and dustballs, but never with one another.

K's theory that the collective unconscious had perceived the impending first world conflict was confirmed by us. Our attitudes mirrored those of the shell-shocked and the gassed she saw among the victims of Verdun when she set out on her fruitless search to find the body of Aristide Marquis. "Just as if they had made the traumas of the war their own. But what is curious is this: if hysterics are bound by reminiscences, all my 'sleepers,' but the Sandman, suffered from the future traumas of perfect strangers."

We all responded to the phases of the moon. Living with us was like living in a clock museum; we'd bellow when the moon was full and low, and cower, winding down, when she'd shown us her horns.

When, later, K ran out of funds, she was forced to sell the spa's extravagant furnishings: the dining-room chairs upholstered in cool leather, the silly canopied beds in which heads of state had battled asthma, the portable tubs posing on gold-dipped feet, the absurdly precious vases and silver. Year after year the rooms were emptied of their treasures so that we, her oblivious wards, as thankless as logs, would survive. She took good care of us. Had it not been for the murderous zealot who notified the Nazis of our existence during the Second War, as late as 1944, it is very likely we would all be alive today. Now these rooms are weather-worn, empty, eerie, and the fissured corridors animated only by the startled eyes of lizards and the eager arrows of their tongues.

The night Sputnik passed overhead, I opened my eyes for the first time in thirty years, and before closing them again for another twenty, I sang a song, Rose's churning song, from start to finish. K managed to catch the refrain:

> *When the Devil comes*
> *take up a stick*
> *and beat, beat, beat him about the horns.*
> *Beat the Devil 'till he calls for his mother;*
> *beat the Devil into white cream*
> *and sweet, sweet butter.*

CHAPTER

13

And now the time has come for me to describe as best I can what surfacing from a fifty-year-long sleep was like. Because it is so hard for me to put to words the feelings which submerged me, I have gone to K's library to read all I can about other beings who died and were reborn.

I have read of the Phoenix which awakens from its ashes a serpent; of Adonis who was kept prisoner in the bowels of the earth; of Attis who unmanned himself. But of all those mythical figures the one I feel closest to is Tammuz of the Sumerians whose name, extraordinarily (at least to me), means: "true son of deep water." He is likened to trees and plants which perish from lack of rain. This I can say about myself: I am parched, arid, the very opposite of young, of rooted, of green. . . .

Perhaps, as Bottlenose believed, all things are but agitation, and time a hollow measure. Those fifty years passed like a clap of thunder. Yet I felt their loss acutely; loss pressed upon my heart like a griffin of bronze.

The question I must answer is this: What awakened me? It was August and an unusually large, full moon was shining. As she wished to gaze upon it in her loneliness, K had not drawn the curtain. She believes some elegant magic took place that night because, after all, this was the same "ogress moon" I had seen as a child in the stairwell. I acknowledge that this explanation is not rational, but I know in my heart of hearts it *was* the orange moon burning in the window which, like a kiss in a fairy-tale, aroused me.

In the beginning the world edged its way into my consciousness. A cry escaped me. When it hit the air it shattered. Doctor Kaiserstiege appeared in a rust-coloured fog.

"Nicolas." She put her hand to my cheek. I recognized her voice and the gesture was tender. "Nicolas." Her voice dissolving darkness. Her glittering tears. "You have been gone a long time." The words unhinged. Letters bobbed in the ocean of my mind like luminous corks.

"May I bring you some milk?" *M* – an abstracted bat rising from the floor to the ceiling, *I* – a wand, *L* – a pharaoh's leg with a toeless foot, *K* – a broken gate. I watched the letters burning in the night, stellar, magical, and took her hand in mind.

Despite Doctor Kaiserstiege's kindness, those first months were a torment. For fifty years my dreams had clothed me like a mantle. Waking tore the fabric of my life. I lay immobile, crushed beneath the weight of my wasted youth. As I gazed at the night sky it seemed the stars were like myself – older and dimmer. In *The Fountains of Neptune* K describes me:

As his dreamed life eclipsed he was seized by vertigo. The fertile island of the mind gave way to a barren and incomprehensible reality. It was as if the spring of his being had run dry.

Although in her eighties, K was still beautiful. The skin of her face was so thin I could see the veins throb at her temples like the rivers of the world seen from the sky. She had a mane of white hair which she pushed from her face with nervous fingers. Her green eyes were orbited with umber; she was far-sighted and could see only distances. Overcome with tenderness I watched her as she sat, her chair ballooning with pillows, bent over an open book. That winter we went through K's favourites; Kafka and Lao Tse, Bachelard and Perrault,

Melville and Freud are the voices of my rebirth. My own voice was an aviary, a froggery, a monkey tree, a caged animal, it croaked and squawked; all the torturous impatience of my confusion tumbling forth like spoiled herrings from a fractured barrel. Now, when I look back, that first winter is a violently coloured jumble of words scented with the plasticene she bought at the *bazar* in thin, ribbed slabs. The first thing I produced as a part of the therapy was an imaginary portrait of Bottlenose.

This figure was followed by another which pleased K so much she had it photographed for the revised edition of the book. It is the figure of a child bent beneath the weight of a woman he carries on his back. K called him "Little Sindbad."

Next I made two figures, a woman and a man, their arms outstretched, beckoning to one another.

"I love you," I mumbled, and gently brought the clay people together for a kiss, "I love you." I pulled them apart and made them embrace with more force. The arms were crooked now; the heads and necks askew. K looked on as I shouted: "I LOVE YOU!" slamming the figures together in a spasmodic convulsion I could not stop. When I had formed a smooth, round ball, I bit into it hungrily.

One morning when I awoke K handed me a cup of hot cocoa and lay eight child's lotto cards across my bed. The printed images were so colourful they seemed ready to ignite: a tiger, a hammer; a firefly, a flaming torch; a windmill, a Buddha; a lighthouse, a mermaid. The mermaid's face and arms were bright pink, her lips scarlet; green scales concealed her breasts and blackened as they tapered to her fin. The sight of her precipitated an explosion of vivid memories: *La Georgette*, the pipe Charlie Dee broke into two, Charlie's murder, the smell of lavender, the smell of fresh sardines.

K pointed to the next card: a handsome devil, his pronged tail coiled about one leg like a snake, a robin with a beetle in its beak; a scorpion, and a bucket; a bee, and a bottle; a wheelbarrow and Louis XIV. With my index finger I caressed the bee, then the devil, and breathed:

"SNAH!"

"The Snail and Shark!" K approved. "And look!" I saw a corkscrew, a church bell; a cooking pot, a helmet; a Gila monster and a barometer; an apron and an apple.

All that morning I looked at the cards and wondered that my life was reduced to potent signs. With my blankets and sheets I made a tent and spent the following weeks in seclusion examining: an eagle, a sphinx, a turkey. . . . K listened at the door hopefully while I gobbled and spoke to the idealized image of an apron. "Rose," I said to it.

Already during this period, curious people would appear at the spa from time to time to see me. Some hoped for a freak, others for a miracle. K would send them away.

"There is only an invalid here," I overheard her say. "A man in need of peace."

It was at that instant that I realized I was no more a little boy, but instead a man.

Each day I looked out the windows at the changing landscape – it took all the courage I had – at the scabs of bark tensing in the shrill air, the famished branches scraping at the skin of the sky; the brown leaves scurrying across the brittle grass; the weeds as furred as spiders squatting beneath an armour of ice.

Each time the crows – always of startling size – lifted their heavy, black bodies to heaven my heart was sheathed in darkness. I saw the elfish rose bushes stripped bare and dancing like bones; the fountains reduced to silence; the gravel paths grim and sodden; I received each storm as a slap across the face; the sun a fist of needles in the eye; the moon a lethal water.

The end of that winter was animated by curious dreams:

"I dreamed a cobbler gave me shoes for walking on water."

"And did you?"

"No. I refused the shoes. I said: 'You've made a dreadful mistake. I asked for shoes for walking *under* the water! Like the Marquis!' "

"Next time you dream I hope he'll offer you both pairs!"

"He gave me a pair for you, K. He said they were made out of Freud's spectacles!"

I remember that after this conversation I spent an hour or two looking into the cracked looking-glass at my aged-infant face, trying to reconcile what I saw there with what I was, or thought I was, my bare feet growing cold on the floor.

When thaw had caused crocuses to detonate all over the grass, I, in a self-pitying mood, complained to K.

"I continue to bark," I said. "I weep round the clock. I am barely able to look at starlight, let alone the light of day. Will I *ever* be normal again?"

"Normal!" she cried. "For Heaven's sake, *Fröschlein*, while you slept the world went mad!" To cheer me, we took a walk, I in my wheelchair and K behind, chatting merrily about the puppets she had seen as a child in the streets of Vienna, the beggar boys turning somersaults for pennies, a trained white rat which shat into a doll's chamber-pot. The description of the rat sent me dreaming.

"If I were strong and rich, I'd form a circus company!" I said. "With trained rats such as that, and dancing dogs, and apes, and elephants – and a yellow-haired dancer riding a woolly buffalo!"

"Which reminds me, Nini – I've been – *we've* been invited to America. When you are all better we will go together to see the buffalo grazing." I hated the idea and told her so.

K wheeled me into town. I had not seen Paradis since my "drowning." We passed the once-wonderful restaurant – now boarded up and barren – where the Marquis had so grandly entertained Rose, Totor, and me.

Time wreaks havoc, there is no doubt about it. Such desolation. . . . The windows filmed with dust as if with smoke. But further on the smells of baking flooded the street and it was at the baker's that an incident occurred which was to affect my cure dramatically: I barked at a woman who prodded me, perhaps not accidentally, with her umbrella. K introduced me to Figuebique, a she-bear of such imperiousness I had to suppress a mad desire to laugh, not because she was funny, but because she was so formidable. I choked, coughed, and succumbed to a species of whinnying.

"You will excuse my friend," said K, "he is only just recovering from a long illness."

"You needn't tell me," Figuebique sneered. "I know who he is: The Last Lunatic."

"And it appears," K countered, magnificent, "that you are The Last Horselaugh." Visibly congested, Figuebique thundered from the shop and slammed the door, its little bell jingling wildly after.

"That was the enemy," K explained gravely. "Now let's go home to tea." Her mood brightened. "I've worked up an appetite."

As she wheeled me back home again, K clued me in to the village and its idiosyncracies.

"Paradis," she said, "is a village inhabited by women who have lost their men repeatedly to war. I know them well. Their lives are like their knitting: introspective, yet mindless; fussy, exacting, repetitive, and pale – tinted by the cheaper dye. Widowed, for the most part, their only comfort is the hairdresser where they exchange the nutshells of their lives. And if God is notoriously absent, they are his ambassadors nonetheless, and call me a heathen because I once took to court a local sorceress who, on the pretext of banishing demons, had starved a man to death. He was suffering from an ulcer.

"They are self-righteous; their knitting consists of cumbersome and useless articles destined for the poor of tropical Africa. And they have made the proprietress of the *bazar* – an infirm creature who was abandoned in the cradle and brought up by charity – their own especial cause. The ugliest among them, she is everybody's favourite.

"Figuebique is the most powerful woman here, though I believe no one likes her; she is far too shrill and domineering. But all admire her as a gifted orator, and at the time of the trial she sided with the witch because she was 'born and bred in Paradis,' and I was the 'outsider.' That a man had died by folly did nothing to temper Figuebique's ardour; you see, her father was the village's only doctor, and I threatened him from the start. His practice relied upon purges (he was of the Old School) and, when they came into vogue, eccentric uses of antibiotics and a smattering of fractured psychoanalytical vocabulary he had learned with the intention of impressing me.

"Once when we met accidentally on the street, Doctor Figuebique bragged about a 'difficult' case he was treating simultaneously for 'ataxia, aphonia, and autocthonous ideas.' The next time we met it was 'dysphagia, dystonia and dystrophy.' Was he memorizing a psychiatric lexicon? 'My patient also suffers from echolalia!' he said. He stood on his toes and hopped, but just a little, in his excitement, 'and ejaculum praecox!' "

After tea we sat together for a time in silence, breathing in the green air and listening to the humming bees; there were so many in the lilac tree that the darkened blossoms vibrated with a kind of self-contained frenzy.

"What," I asked, feeling strong and peaceful, "do you know about my mother?"

"Odille! She was an enchantress of sorts; a child inhabiting the body of a grown person."

"As I!"

"As you. . . ." For a time she did not speak. "There is much turmoil ahead, Nini," she said at last. "Odille's story is . . . extravagant. With each day you are growing stronger. We have all the time in the world ahead of us. Reflect upon what was her apparent loveliness and loneliness – both of a startling character. And the fact that she had the heart of a child, a child who had run away. I could never learn from what."

"And soon . . . you will tell me more?"

"I will tell you everything I know."

"Last night," I said, all at once remembering, "I had a terrible dream. I was alone in Rose's kitchen. On the floor lay a lid which I was forbidden to touch. But I seized it by the handle and lifted it anyway. Under, I saw a deep pit; it seemed to fall away from my eyes forever."

"*Fröschlein*," K squeezed my hand. "You have had that dream before. What happened next?"

"Rose came and put back the lid."

"A luminous dream," K said.

Suddenly I was angry. "You are like Rose in my dream," I cried, "putting back! BACK! BACK! The lid."

"The day you no longer need wheels to get about," K promised, "the day you are able to take long, thoughtful walks alone, that day I will tell you what I know about Odille, your lost, your damned, your beautiful mother."

That night in my room I walked with my hands to the walls. Around and around I went in the moonlight, despite the pain in my legs which was so unbearable I fell to the floor again and again, and as a dog worries a bone, gnawed upon the flesh of my own naked arm.

CHAPTER

14

"I wish to see the city," I said one day to Doctor Kaiserstiege. "I wish to see and know everything which touches upon my atrophied past."

K said she feared the shock would be too much for me, but after reflection concluded that the head-on collision could cause a fusion, as if that impact might melt the skins of those alien entities: past and present. Because the "present" in my case was simultaneously the "future," she warned that "to see the city would be like attempting to mate a tiger with a bear."

"It was eerie," K said as she soaped down the Peugeot prior to our departure, "how as soon as you were installed deep-dreaming at the spa, all those others started showing up. As if that day out on the lake they had fallen into that potent water with you. You were traumatized by the past and they by the future (which was swiftly becoming the present). For example – have I told you this? At his worst the cobbler would throw himself into the air as if he had been hit in the gut by a grenade and cry:

" 'There are pieces of me everywhere! Someone fetch them! Fetch them quick! Catgut! A needle! A needle!' So that I knew the shoes he sewed fulfilled a neurotic need. 'Ovens!' the lovers shrieked at one another. 'Ovens! Ovens!' I had to wait years to understand what that was all about.

"One of my patients tied a colander to his face – to protect himself from the poisons in the air – and another wore a cooking pot to protect his skull from shrapnel. Ah!" K smiled her gentle, ironic smile. "We've become a race of Tweedle-dees and dums, and the black crow, you know, is only ourselves." I had not yet read *Alice* and so had no idea what she was talking about. I held my peace, attempting, for that day at least, not to badger her, as was my compulsion, with questions.

My own childhood favourites had been Jules Verne and H.G. Wells. In K's Peugeot I saw a time machine, a rocket to the future-present. But as we left the familiar green spaces of the countryside behind and approached the city, excitement ceded to anxiety, and anxiety to panic.

"Back!" I barked. "Turn back! Back! Back!"

"I'll take you to the museum," K cried, inspired, precipitating us around a hairpin curve and up a one-way street. "I've been told there are photographs of the city as it was before the wars. What a fool I was not to think of this earlier!" We sped past a bank fronted with green mirrors, and a municipal building of aluminum.

I think now that had I awakened two decades earlier I would have been less shaken. Then I would have seen a wasteland, the port a ragged lip of rubble, the breakwater in collapse, the shards of ships stranded in dismal heaps along the beach, great mounds of muck thrown up from the deep belly of the sea. I would have seen the destruction of all that I had loved. But what I saw was worse because it denied memory. Nothing remained that I could recognize.

K explained that if the city had survived the First War, the Second had destroyed it utterly. Machines had scraped the rubble from the blasted earth to create a smooth, uniform surface upon which the new city, reduced, or so it seemed, to minimal signs, and dominated by tragic forms K called "residential superblocks," had been built by the very same industrialists who had made fortunes in the wars, producing shells and grenades and mustard gas in the First; and tanks and the packaging for tank parts and pharmaceuticals in the Second. K called this city "Amnesia." When I said I longed to return to the spa's charming ruins and the village of Paradis which – but for a television set which materialized grinning and winking each evening in the darkest corner of the café – remained unchanged, she said:

"There's not much left for those who long for Paradise! Soon all the cities of the world will look just like Amnesia!"

The museum was a pyramid of cinder blocks badly stained by rain. We entered it by way of a diminishing funnel, which added to my feeling of unease, and by a brightly illuminated escalator which took us to the utmost peak of what proved to be a cone. K rolled me out upon a descending spiralling ramp; the pyramid's inner structure was modelled on the towers of Babylon.

I hated those curved, windowless walls, the felted silence; above all, I wondered about the spaces between the cone's outer walls and the inside of the pyramid. That ambiguous void disturbed me so much that for many weeks after I obsessively drew little pictures of pyramids containing cones. The place still haunts my dreams even now; it makes its appearance as a necromantic mountain, and its lost spaces are my lost youth.

As K wheeled me down a carpeted incline, I devoured the slices and fragments of my phantom city: the port, the fishing boats as they had been, the rugged coast, its gulls, its mist, its fishermen in slickers, and the charming streets; street-hawkers holding up dolls, and frying pans and freshly dipped candles, and freshly baked bread.

"Look!" I cried. "Here's Saint Peter's fountain! And the barrister's beyond – and K! The junk shop! The junk shop *window!*" She helped me to my feet and held my hand as I squinted at the wall, attempting to find meanings in that clotted fog.

"If we had a glass," she began, "but no – the window is too small and, besides, everything is muddled by the fountain's spray."

I trembled with excitement and pointed to a precious image of the Snail and Shark's façade.

"The negative's printed back, back, BACKWARDS!" I managed to sputter.

"*Coffee black as Satan*," K read aloud, slowly deciphering the text. "What a wonderful Devil! These pictures are a gold mine, yes! But calm yourself, *Liebling*, pull yourself together. No need to make a spectacle of yourself." I barked once in agreement, shrugged apologetically, then struck out at a label neatly pinned beneath a picture of the Snail and Shark's front room titled: "The Galaxy."

"But – it's not, not, NOT! The Galaxy!" I shouted, furious. "The Galax-ax-AX! Galaxy was a tiny place," I wept, "overcrowded with a little stage. The stage was dark" – I pushed my fists into my eyes, beginning to dream – "dark most of the time. But once in a great while there was a performance of some kind. Totor took me one Sunday afternoon when Rose was at a funeral.

"There was a *chanteuse*, a tiny, golden-haired girl named Tina who wore nothing but a pair of paper wings and a pink leotard pinned with roses. She sang a song about heartbreak and kicked up her heels at the end of each stanza. Having never before seen tights I believed she had webbed toes. I heard the Cod's wife say later that Tina was *passée*, but I thought her wonderful and for many months dreamed about her feet, her *very* pink skin, the rose blooming on her breasts. It was Maximinole who rent the mystery when he said that if Tina wore tights she also wore a wig! Tina was *old*! And I'd believed she was a child – not much older than myself!"

We came to a second picture of the fountain – a close-up of Saint Peter capped with bird droppings. I recalled the priest's filthy ankles as he lifted his skirts and splashed into the water to thrash the Saint into obedience. We saw pictures of the canneries, the women looking overworked and strained in their aprons weighty with oil. I wept to think that as I had slept all this had disappeared forever; that these people were for the most part dead, their bones baking in the earth. I had a dreadful vision then: I saw – rising from that place where the city of my childhood had been – a pyramid of skulls pointing to the sky's unfathomable dome of blackest night; the world snatched and throttled in the dung-clotted fist of time.

In profound crisis I cried out:

"Odille! She's *here*! Somewhere – I know she's here." And then: "There's Rose! It's *Rose*!" Together we squinted at the faded image, a market scene watermarked and creased. But was this Rose's firm little figure sagging to the left beneath the irresistible weight of a very large basketed fish? Or was it someone else?

"It *is* Rose," I insisted, although unsure, for the woman was wearing clogs and Rose always wore shoes, not clogs "like Naked Ignorance!" No, I decided close to tears, it isn't Rose.

K was gazing at the pictures hungrily. Somewhere in that confusion of faces and figures, salt-stained and standing in shadow, or stooped and squinting in the sun, she might see Aristide Marquis. I dried my eyes on my sleeve, and together we examined the faces of the men; as out on the breakwater they sat together mending nets in the haze, or on the decks of fishing boats stood beside boiling cauldrons, their identities decomposing in steam or reduced to a smear as they danced in celebration on the beach.

"To see his face again . . ." she murmured. To my astonishment it seemed to me that she – the fervent atheist – was praying. But there was no one as tall, or as beautiful as he, and clearly, no one as black.

"Many of these photographs are very old," K said, "taken even before our time. It was the First War that changed the faces and figures of the women and the men, and the face of the city. Until then things had drifted along unchanged for decades, long strings of decades. . . ."

We were both drawn then to a young woman's face – a portrait of considerable technical skill. She was standing against a folding screen, her hands behind her back, and she was wearing a strange assortment of rags artfully pinned. She was uncommonly pretty. I wondered aloud if this could be my mother.

"Yes," K agreed. "I imagine her this way. I imagine your father would have captured this expression – a mood that, perhaps, no one else would have perceived. Your father would have caught her wistfulness."

"My father?" I was confused.

"Your father was a photographer."

For a time I considered this in silence. "My father was a photographer, and *she*," I whispered in awe, "she could be . . . *Odille*." I had risen to my feet unaided, and my heart was madly beating.

"Yet she doesn't look anything like you, Nini," K reconsidered. "See – the eyes so far apart and her mouth large and down-turned. And she's so dark, so exotic looking, really. She looks Latin, Spanish – Arab, perhaps. . . . She *is* lovely! Haughty if sad. . . . There's a hint of malicious laughter lurking in those oval eyes. . . . It's clear she's seen too much, poor child, too soon. Then again – perhaps you take after your father."

"I do!" I told her about the photograph I had found in Rose's drawer. "But, K – maybe there is *something* in my face like hers?"

"Well – let's see you!" she said, turning me around and gazing at me earnestly. I do not know what she saw, but now her own eyes filled with tears.

"Oh, Nicolas!" she sobbed, taking me into her arms and holding me. "When the past is . . . is . . . *only scraps of paper!*" I had never seen this strong woman weep and I was shaken.

"K!" I barked wildly, clutching at her. "K! K!"

The curator came running, angered and perplexed, and suggested – if only by his agitated presence – that we be on our way.

K wheeled me past the pictures of both world wars: the battleships, the bombings, the city's disarticulated skeleton. I saw a barefoot boy stumbling past a gutter filled with bodies, and thought I saw myself.

There were deep windows filled with life-size manikins dressed as Rose, Totor, and I had dressed, and cans from the cannery, and household articles including carved spoons which had once belonged to fishermen. I dared not look at any of these things too closely.

"All I have of the Marquis is one letter," K explained as we rushed away, "and it is a letter he did not even write. And all you have of your father is the memory of a photograph. And of your mother –"

"The picture of a perfect stranger," I said decisively, knowing as I did that if the beautiful girl in rags was not my mother, she was the closest I'd ever get to her. "The letter –"

"The letter was written by a friend the Marquis had made in the trenches. The place was called Verdun."

We had come to the bottom of the ramp. Above and beyond, the museum spiralled in all its felted luminosity. The funnel of the exit, also brightly lit, stretched out before us. We were in an alcove dwarfed by an outsize anchor.

"Would you like me to read the letter to you?" K took a worn wallet of red leather from her purse and opened it. As the letter was very old she unfolded it carefully.

"*Madame,*" K began, "*there is so much death here every day the dead cannot be counted. We live in troughs slippery with greenish mud and excrement oozing up from the Devil knows* where. *We cannot believe that this is happening to us; that we were born for this. We forget who we are, Madame. It's hard to believe that we are human beings, even. Better to be a bug in this filth; a dung beetle's paradise it is. Better to be a worm because our minds are sticky with anger.*

"*And I am so afraid. Everywhere I look I see craters where blood pools. And I weep. Because I am up to my neck in crime. Because I am caught like a sinner in a net of fire. Because the air I breathe is sharp with the splinters of trees and wire and the small, hot particles of my friends.*

"*Above all I weep because the Marquis is gone, enchantment is gone, and where he stood there is a hole, a great hole at the heart of the world. And all the wishful substance of our love can do nothing.*

"And all the wishful substance . . ." K sighed. "He was Eros, come to walk the earth. He quickened me and everything he touched. . . . The wars killed Eros," said Venus Kaiserstiege. She folded the letter and put it away.

CHAPTER

15

My life is an enchantment, not a fairy-tale. I am no Sleeping Beauty animated by a kiss, but a chronically ugly duckling hatched thanks to the perpetual ministrations of a dedicated doctor, or, as Doctor Kaiserstiege insists, "liberated at the completion of some obscure cycle of the psyche."

That I awoke an old man is true and untrue. Sleep had inhibited aging so that the skin of my face is smooth and my body, if stiff and prey to the odd muscular tremor, is slender. There is something uncommonly soft and feminine about my appearance, though I treasure a beard which I keep neatly trimmed. I am very tall – well over six feet – and walk (I am beginning to walk now) with a slight stoop. I have a large nose, somewhat beaked, and this is fortunate as it imparts a much desired ruggedness to my features. I walk every day; I am attempting to bake my face into an outdoorsman's leathery mask. Consequently my nose is always peeling.

I sometimes think that if I could pock my skin, artificially age it, I could look like another dreamer, the American statesman Abraham Lincoln. You see – it is not my homeliness which embarrasses me, but the symptom of my infirmity: uncanny youthfulness. This and the diminutive size of my hands.

Returning one afternoon from a stroll in the gardens, I found K sitting in her study sipping tea. The sweetness of her greeting filled my heart with happiness; feeling strong and peaceful I said: "Now, tell me about Odille."

Doctor Kaiserstiege's story begins in September of 1914 when she went to the city to "hunt down clues, and," she admitted, "Aristide Marquis. The tender fearlessness of that man's eyes had captivated me. I desired two things simultaneously: the knowledge of the trauma which had lead to your own self-abandonment and further carnal knowledge of the Marquis, or, in other words, my own self-abandonment.

"The war was on. The port was full of immobile boats because so many men had been sent to the front. I explored the streets until I found Rose and Totor's house.

"I pleaded with Rose to talk about the past but she said only: 'The tongue's best kept between the teeth and slops in the pail,' and other such nonsense. Totor was an empty husk, Nini, bewildered by what had happened, and in pain. Visibly his heart was breaking. I knew later that he blamed himself for letting you go out on the water with someone *who did not know*. You see, in his mind, Odille had grown into mythical proportions, Ogress and Vouivre combined."

"My mother! An Ogress-Vouivre!" It came to me that the stories Toujours-Là had told me had all conveyed this. I said as much to K.

"Your mother left so many stories behind her! And *songs*, Nini. She had sparked the imaginations of everyone. She did so much harm, but *unintentionally*. I don't believe she was evil. But only a child ruled by desire. Her need, her loneliness, must have been so implacable, so exigent. . . ."

I thought of my own need, my own loneliness, and shivered.

"Totor and I left Rose behind in her kitchen stirring a custard," K continued. "The whole street smelled of vanilla."

"I remember so well," I said then, my mind reeling with the memory of Rose's kitchen, "that smell!"

"We walked out to the breakwater," she went on, "and

stood in silence for hours. He wept; he was convinced you were lost to him forever. It was true: you were lost to *him* forever. I realized then that he was a very superstitious man because when he spoke he said: 'It's her curse! That damned Odille! She's stolen Nini!' And he sobbed. I wondered: Odille? A *curse*? But could get no more out of him. As it was getting cold and wet we went to the Ghost for something hot."

"The Ghost! Is it still there!"

"That was then, Nicolas. You know the city is gone now."

"The Ghost," I said, "is gone!" Even today it continues to exist with such vibrancy in my mind. "And then?" I pressed her, eager to know more. "What happened then?"

"Totor pushed open the door," K continued, "and we saw the Marquis barefoot on the bar. He was juggling six empty bottles. He saw us and caught them one by one. Then he handed them to the Cod's wife – who was scowling at me – and leapt to the floor." For several instants she was silent.

"There was – how can I say it – a *tension* between us. As if our hearts were strung upon the same, taut wire. I had difficulty speaking. Breathing that potent air was difficult enough. I believe I may have sighed."

"And he?"

"His eyes smiled!" I nodded; I knew. "Totor left us then. He vanished. He took *La Georgette* out to sea, and the fog, his old companion, claimed him. Totor was embraced by the weather and the water one last time. Perhaps he saw suicide – for that is what it was – as an act of atonement, or a way of placating the angry spirit of Odille." She paused. "I have always feared that it was my insistence to speak about the past that precipitated Totor's death. I believed that if I knew the truth I might save you all. I should have known. But everything had lost its place. Order was abolished and with it distance. The world had become a jumble of sensations. When one is in love, Nicolas, the world swarms." When I reddened she squeezed my hand.

"It is not too late for you to know love."

Agitated, I barked softly. K pretended not to notice.

"I explained to the Marquis why I had come; that I needed to learn about your past; that I needed to know what had happened, *exactly what had happened*. He had been untouched by the stories and the songs. He was intact – as if he inhabited another space, another dimension. Filth did not stick to him! But the Cod's wife knew. She overheard me – she'd been hovering around us jealously; I thought her offensive and absurd: the sooty eyebrows and rouged cheeks! She took hold of Aristide's shoulder defiantly, wanting me to think he was her property. She said: 'Take her to Toujours-Là!'

"I thrilled at this! Because as you slept you had so often breathed those two mysterious words. It had never occurred to me this was someone's name. Toujours-Là! Always there! The man you can be sure to find, day or night, haunting the darkest recesses of the bar. 'You know him!' I cried. 'Where can I find him?'

"The Cod's wife gave me an address on a torn piece of paper. I took her hand to thank her, and all at once I saw how good she was. I felt ashamed for despising her, her desperate attempts at beauty, her hand posed with hopeless love upon Aristide's shoulder. She looked into my eyes then, surprised but pleased. And we were friends, accomplices.

" 'I must warn you,' the Cod's wife said, 'he's up there drunk and dying. Sometimes he's sane and sometimes he isn't. Don't believe everything he tells you.' "

"Where was he?" I asked.

"There was a room," K began, "up a stairway. The whole thing listing, rotting –"

"I remember!"

"You'd been there?" K asked.

"He took me there!"

"Who? The Marquis?"

"No!" I answered. "Toujours-Là! He took me there. To

show me . . . to show me. . . ." The incandescent figures of the Cod's wife and Gilles and Gillesbis leapt up from the grottoes of my memory. As the vision bore down upon me, I doubled over sputtering like a baby. When much later I could speak again, and K asked me what I had seen and what I had felt, I told her that above all I had felt *shame*.

Doctor Kaiserstiege did not continue with her story until several days later, and then only after I had assured her I was well enough to listen. Of all the stories I had ever heard, hers interested me the most. After all, it was, in fact, my own. However, I should make it clear that this *récit*, written down several years later, is, in part, the fruit of a reconstruction which includes her notes and passages from her diaries now in my keeping. At the time, K did not, and wisely so, repeat *everything* the old soaker had told her.

"The Cod's wife had been caring for him," K began, "and the room and bedclothes were clean enough although the air was foul. He was dying. His liver was so swollen I wondered that he continued to survive. At first he refused to let me near him.

"Aristide said: 'She wants to know about Odille.'

"And something strange came to pass. He seemed to dream. When he awakened, he spoke in a fever, extravagantly, for close to an hour.

" 'Odille was wild,' Toujours-Là began, 'the wildest of all women; she was the flame that never dies. . . .

" 'She appeared from nowhere, from some hellish paradise and the city was swept up in the storm of that woman's thighs, the tempest of her eyes; she was a whirlpool! And we – we was all sucked in!

" 'She was a'ways on fire; the air crackled where'er she moved an' Odille was a walker, she walked all over, in every hole and corner and to the four winds – looking to be laid!

Odille fucked fierce! She fucked to outdo Satan; she screwed to try God's patience and man's faith in the divine.

" 'Sailors would come to port and set right out looking for Odille at the Ghost, the Galaxy, and the Snail and Shark.' He laughed, and his laughter was a rattling hiss.

" 'She'd do it everywhere! Why! She'd do it all over Hell!' He groaned and his lips were flecked with foam. 'I swear: THE FOG STILL SMELLS OF THAT SLUT'S CUNT! MIX ME!' Toujours-Là rose up from the bed, shouting, 'MIX ME! MIX ME! *Mix me!*' he pleaded, 'a wee *panaché*, for the love of God.' He fell back, perspiring heavily. I bathed him and straightened his sheets as Aristide went over to the nearest bar for a bottle of absinthe.

" 'She had a *juice* on her, see,' Toujours-Là whispered, 'like a fine old barrel-cured whisky. Drove men into con-convulsions! She was our cu-cult, our ceremony, our sa-sacra-sacrament. I'M DYING!' he shouted. 'I'LL DIE TELLING SOME CUNT DOCTORESS ABOUT ODILLE FOR CHRISSAKES!

" 'Once you had Odille,' he gurgled, 'you a'ways wanted more. Her crack weren't wide enough for all of us at once so they was plenny of fights. Men got hurt. She had a favourite, a Hindoo who was murdered in a brawl down at the Sna-Sna-Snark; left his blood all over the walls an' floor. Some said jealousy had turned that man's blood to acid, that the mirror behind the bar was foxed by the Hindoo's blood. . . . To love that woman was to love self-immolation! I never understood it, but Odille was devastated by her lover's death. Though she'd had worlds of men! She was a screwer, see, a threader; Odille was a whore. They was a song: *She was our sea of trouble, our wa-water of li-life; all our dirty weather; everyman's wife.* . . . Argh! I can't recall the rest. Something about . . . stars. . . .

" 'I was sayin' we fought for her which was absh . . . absurd 'cause all of us could, would, or *had* had her! She did it like life depended on it! Like the world would stop still if she stopped fucking! And yet, when her Hindoo lay dying on the floor, she wept! She was blue for weeks. You understand' – he swallowed hard – 'I loved her. I guess we all loved Odille. She poisoned our existence. WHERE'S MY DRINK? WHERE'S THAT NIGGER? SHIT!'

" 'You watch your mouth,' the Marquis said, returning with an armful of bottles, 'else I serve this *panaché* as a purge.' Toujours-Là watched greedily as absinthe and mint syrup transformed themselves into the lethal jade he adored.

" 'I a'ways liked you,' Toujours-Là said, as he reached for the glass. But he was shaking too badly to take it. The Marquis cradled his head and gently poured the drink down the dying man's throat. Toujours-Là swallowed, coughed, wheezed, dribbled, and sighed.

" 'I never dreamed I'd be extremely unctioned by a black man,' he managed to sputter before sinking into sleep.

"The Cod's wife joined us sometime in the night.

" 'I will tell you what my husband saw,' she said, and she sat down at the foot of the bed. She described the crime as the Cod had seen it: the sun, the water, Odille, Thomas, the horned photographer, and you – the infant who was about to be thrust from the garden forever. Startled by your mother's screams, you awakened in time to see your father's face taken by the water; his body slowly sinking beneath the surface of the sea. You know the sea to be an Ogress, Nicolas; did she not eat your father?' "

The day Doctor Kaiserstiege repeated the Cod's wife's story to me, there in the spa's weedy garden, I saw myself as if from a great distance; saw a puppet-infant, its head stuffed with shrieks, bewitched by water, the fissured, riddled water – and reaching out for that place where a beloved face had been swallowed whole like a small, smooth stone. I saw the planet of the past rise like a sphere of black glass, and I knew in my heart why fifty years before I had tumbled from *La Puce d'Eau* into my own reflection. . . .

K picked up the story then where she had left off:

"Toujours-Là woke up, and, raising himself and clawing at the air, cried: 'Odille! I've not . . . done! She were . . . destitute. Never a penny. 'Twas the men'd buy her supper, her rags. She had these sailors' queer ideas of what wha . . . waz pretty – a Spanish shawl, a Japanese kimono, a brocade dress bought in some fly-shit *souk*. . . . So, she's sitting in the Ghost one day when thish fun-house figure comes tripping in, a landlubber green as a caterpillar, not a sailor, jus' a masturbator, a frog-arsed photographer thish was, see, wanting to immortalize the Ghost, the Cod's wife, the boys, even the bottles of toxicants behind the bar. He had these crazy notions. "There's a war coming," he'd say, "and after, nothing will be th' same. Time is telescoping," he'd say; "Time's twistin' the world outta shape." He took pictures of all the bars in town, the fishermen, fishwives, and whores. This was one dough-faced snoop, if you wants to know, talking Art (well bless my fart), but in truth as nosy as an elephant in a harem. When he sees Odille sipping schnapps, he wants her picture, too, and she's pleased. She even smiles for the first time in weeks. He buys her a first-class meal with wine and sherbet! She starts sittin' for him in all the places she's been laid, only he doesn't know that. And one day in the Snail an' Shark she takes off all her clothes. Poor sod! He gets down on his knees and kisses her feet and won't thread her 'till she promises to marry him.

" 'Now Totor is up the coast with the lobster boat, *Karl Marx*, and by the time he gets back, the photographer has proposed to Odille. Totor's so good he sees no evil in the news, tells us his nephew – that milky, bespectacled dainty – has "tamed the vigorous tart." *Vigorous tart!* Our own Goddess of Fesaninity! Our own Demoness Fornicatress! Yesh! Odille and the photographer is married a month and she's already fuckin' Thomash! Thas why Thomash a'ways claimed the boy waz his!"

" 'But Odille, she insisted that the father waz the short-sighted photographer. They fought about it, Thomash an' Odille, an' maybe that day out on the water that's what all the shouting was about. . . . What the Cod saw wi' his li'l tele-scopical . . . through the glass . . . through the glass.' Tou-jours-Là put his hand to his throat and squeezed. Then he laughed; he laughed until he coughed, choked, spat up a thread of green bile, and, exhausted, once more fell asleep.

"Those were his last lucid moments. That night as Death raked him over her bed of cold bones he raved, shrieked the names of 'shit-arsed captains, King Squid and the Harpoon,' and 'shit-hole ships: the *Nautilus*, the *Adam's Rib*, and the *Typhoon*,' and all the 'shit-house whores' he'd ever had: 'Hairy Cyclops, Oyster Roxanne, Salt Sally'; and all his favourite 'piss-ant poisons,' the ones that tie the testicles in knots, or tear the optic nerve to shreds, and suck reason from the mind like marrow from a bone. He belched, he brayed canticles of agony and hymns of fever; the room reverberated with his final gasps. Then, rising with a shudder, Toujours-Là shouted for the last time: 'A FINGER FOR THE CAPTAINS! A FINGER FOR THE WHORES! A FINGER! A FINGER! FOR GOD!'

"As the Cod's wife closed the dead man's eyes, the Marquis sang the song he had heard the sailors sing at the Ghost, the Galaxy, and the Snail and Shark. When he threw back his head, the tendons of his neck were traced in blue shadow. I never forgot the words:

" 'She was our sea of trouble
   our water of life;
   she was all our dirty weather;
   everyman's wife.

She was all our shipwrecks,
black moon and evil star.

Yet she shined upon our lives
like the lamp above the bar.

She drank us down like water –
our mischief was her cure; she!
Our mastaba and our lure!
O holiest of terrors –
strongest drink and reddest meat –
the wasp's nest of that woman's sex
was sweet.' "

CHAPTER

16

Winter came, windy and wet. Mornings, K read in her study while I sat in bed meditating upon the lithographer's observable universe, my lotto cards, redolent of fixative and ink. K had uncovered more cards in the *bazar*; I now owned ten sets: six hundred and forty images.

I played a game of solitaire, obscuring a card's eight pictures with eight others pulled blind from the pack of cardboard duplicates. When I turned these face up I saw, often with a shudder of delight, what chance had brought together: hawk and spyglass; cossack and compass; Cyclops and Manticore; ferret and wasp. Memory book and music book, these images produced a concordant chiming, if only I looked at them long enough.

At winter's end, a violent wind ripped through the roof of the spa. It tore off dozens of slate tiles and scattered them across the gardens and lawns. Chimney bricks plunged into the attic. These minor disasters coincided with renewed entreaties from America; K was being urged to offer a series of conferences on the theme of what she called, "metamusic."

She was tempted by the change, and by the money – far more than what we needed for repairs. She insisted I go along. Because of her book I had become famous; it troubled her that I was not eager to share in the limelight.

"Illness is self-containing," she argued. "And shrinking from the world only causes it to shrink. Aren't you curious? We are to take a jet-propelled airplane." I cringed. "Would you prefer to sail?"

I preferred not to go at all. America was at war in Indochina. I wanted nothing to do with a country at war.

"Would you sleep through all wars, *Lauschen*," K teased me gently, "and never wake up? Do you wish to be God again, Nicolas? Simultaneously dreaming and being the world?" I did.

We are all ghosts, I thought, reflecting upon those photographs of vanished people and places I had seen at the museum. As K and I speak together in what we call the "present," is my past any less real than hers?

"I just need to think," I told her, "to continue my little games of remembering." In fact, my decision to remain behind was hastened by a desperate desire to dream. And to dream without a witness.

K sensed the danger. She said: "The world is populated with living beings, dearest, each exceptional, each unique. Therein lies its richness. Now that you have joined us, let love lead you. It is the best the world, any world, has to offer. Yet –" she considered, "solitude can be nurturing and I can understand that you are eager to see the world with your own eyes. Without a meddlesome old lady in your way! Only, promise to remember always: the password is life."

She then recounted a brutal incident from the Second War. In the spring of 1944, a Nazi officer kicked apart the spa's beautiful door of cut glass. As K stood on the threshold in her nightgown, trembling "not with fear, Nini, but anger." The officer saluted her and said: "Murder is the password." But he did not kill her. Instead, he tied her to a chair and gagged her with a handkerchief into which he had spat. And he blindfolded her.

Then needles were thrust into the veins of her "sleepers."

In her mind's eye she could see the poison enter the skin just under the cobbler's ear. She saw the lovers, still clinging together, collapse like a house of cards to the ballroom floor with a hiss. She felt her sleepers' lives drift away one by one, as if a flock of birds had taken wing; she could hear Death beating the air with wings.

A great fire was set in the driveway. Even K's rare zoological books were destroyed – those with the hand-tinted plates she had so often described to me in detail. At the foot of the stairs the sand had melted into a pool of glass fantastically coloured by the ashes of a pygmy princess, her hair in spiralled plaits, straddling the neck of a blue elephant; of a woolly rhinoceros caked with red dust; of pomegranate trees swarming with butterflies; of purple rats knotted together by their tails. There were other things just as wonderful: copulating serpents, their scales and eyes set like gems; and a toad as large as a man's head whose voice could be heard thirty miles away. A tiny figure stood on a mountain, listening.

Only one book survived. It was the book which precipitated K's initial vision of "metamusic," so essential to her understanding of my case. Its name is *The Virtuous Abyss*, and it is described at length in *The Fountains of Neptune*.

Her recollection of this terrible night evoked a memory of my own, which surfaced in the form of an evil dream the night preceding K's departure for America. This memory I described in detail at breakfast, the last meal we were to share for many months.

Rose had owned a cat. One day I came into the kitchen just as it was giving birth beside the hearth. Her kittens slid from her body, contained in pearly sacks. A crimson cluster was caught to each, like the corals of some fabulous sea. It had seemed to me that the kittens had been laid, like soft, translucent eggs; precious eggs like those described in a fairy-tale. Beneath the glistening shell I had seen them palpitate and twitch.

One by one Rose lay the kittens in a large mixing bowl she had set outside the kitchen door. There she had made a nest of lethal rags soaked in ether. The births were swift and easy and the kittens never once awakened from their sleep.

K became very concerned.

"Nicolas!" she cried. "How I wish we'd had a chance to talk about this before!"

"For weeks the cat searched for them," I continued, "calling and calling."

The cab began to beep impatiently in the driveway, ready to take Doctor Kaiserstiege to the train for Paris. She held me close for a long moment.

"You are my only child," she said, her eyes wet with tears. I, too, was deeply moved and only then aware that *it was happening*: K was leaving me. I kissed her wet cheeks and in that instant realized as I never had before, that this ancient woman, so loving and so strong, had been my life, my breath, my voice.

And what if, I thought with panic, I am only a thing of her own mind? My confusion was such that I hid my face in my hands and did not see her enter the cab; nor did I see her wave goodbye. When I looked again she was gone, as if she and the cab had been transmuted to dust.

After her departure I peeled off my clothes and soaked for the rest of the day in *das charybdische Sprudelbad* – K's celebrated tub, the one the Americans call "The Kaiser Milkshake." The tub's shell-shaped womb is the perfect environment for those who need comforting, and the sound of the foam – churned to a milky froth and sent cascading over the body from feet to chest in the manner of a gently pounding surf – has a soothing effect. Like a hermit crab soaking in a secret compartment of an empty shell deep in the body of the sea, I lay in the tub and thought how I might one day expand to occupy the spa's every tub and room and furnish them with what K calls "an active, an inventive life."

Yet, contradictory feelings submerged me. I suffered pangs of self-loathing for what I feared to be a morbid need for solitude. I felt light, exhilarated, and even giddy because – aside from the housekeeper who would prepare my lunch before leaving for the day – there would be no one to account to but myself.

Soon the postcards K sent from Manhattan and then Dallas were pinned to the bathroom wall: cities of glass and metal, which the steam curled at the edges.

A penny, K scribbled on the backs of each, *for your thoughts.*

I answered: *Often I see the world dissolve beneath a great weight of dust which falls softly like a sooty snow. I hear it sifting down from space – just as if a gigantic hourglass had ruptured. Is Time a mouth spitting soot in my direction?*

Dearest, she replied, *don't be so hard on yourself. After all, you've cheated Time most of your life. The dreamer's clock barely ticks at all!*

Sometimes, I wrote to her, *the world appears to me as did my father's face beneath the water – as an object coveted beyond a dust-laden pane of glass.*

So much is inaccessible! K answered. *And the mind is constantly appealed to by Mysterious Others riding swift and thin as atoms in the air. We brood and would take a deeper look. And we dream. Dreams are our networks to a faster, brighter world. . . .*

Sometimes, I wrote back, *the junk shop window is wiped clean by a fairy hand and I see the world shining like a newly laid egg. I look into a forest of edible trees rooted in rock candy and recall what the world was like when all its maps were charted by Totor. How it unfolded, untouched by bitterness; how it stretched, marvellous and untried, to the horizon. Even the Cod's wife's pewter bar was miraculous then. And the Snail and Shark's foxed mirror.*

My dearest Nicolas, she wrote, *how not to brood? The spa's walls are stained by rain, and every ceiling is as split and swollen as the spine of a moulting snake. The floors are encrusted with grime and the husks of insects collect in drifts beneath the stairs. Americans complain incessantly of their allergies; fortunately neither you nor I are allergic to dust!*

When the wind blows through the broken windows those bodies scatter, I wrote to K, *and I see maps of mandibles and wings! Or some plan for the making of a man, or a model of the gardens of Eden. I am fashioning myself of this dust and of the mud I make with my tears. I would build us a moat of tears!*

CHAPTER

17

In dreams light and shadow do not depend upon the sun and moon, but have lives of their own. Ominous hazes give way to the blazing light of midday; it is the emotions which illuminate the world, and a day which begins at night may end at noon. Reflected upon the face of the adulterer, the friend, the stranger, midnight has the same luminosity as noon. Dreams, like the cinema, favour artificial light.
         – from The Fountains of Neptune

Each morning in *das charybdische Sprudelbad* I anticipated my possession of the spa – just as I imagine a man looks forward to a new mistress, investing his expectation with unrestricted fantasy. I wondered if Doctor Kaiserstiege had known that I wanted to be alone not only because I was ready to function as an autonomous being, but because I intended to plunge back into an ocean of phantoms – would she have gone away?

You see: I wanted to distil the essence of the past. To recreate its transient substance. I entertained this possibility: that the present is suspended between two vibrations, and Time a concerted music which can be captured just by reaching for it with the mind.

I wanted to dwell upon the past unimpeded. I wanted to dream again and just as shamelessly. Ever since awakening I had felt like a gravity-bound alien dropped to Earth from a lighter world. I had come to look upon my passage through limbo as a state of grace. (Later, much later, K admitted that she had been aware of the danger. "But it was what you wanted, Nicolas. And it was time for you to live, as you wished, and *with risks*.")

Empty rooms have their character – rather like a patient who has left all effects behind and lies naked beneath a white sheet, stripped down to the self's essential bone, waiting for health or for death. The rooms spoke to me, sometimes in whispers, sometimes in groans. I heard them reverberate with screams and shuddered to hear them weep.

As the perforated wheel of the constellations turned, I attempted to people the spa with all the passion of my untried heart and the freakish power of my brain. I began to feel at ease in the spa's sprawling maze. *The shell does not shrink*, I wrote to K, *the crab gets fatter*.

This was my stage and these my props: an obelisk lost among the trees; a staircase carved of shadow; the worn marble of abandoned floors soaking up a landscape reflected in windows desperately in need of washing. An empty cabinet smelling faintly of cordials. An attic as vast as a cathedral. The hot cubbyholes of chambermaids. Balconies green with wind-sewn weeds, their rotting balustrades. Overgrown topiaries battling above the quiet pool where I saw my own reflection as beaked as any heron's. The gazebo where – on a life-saving whim of K's – I once slept tranquilly as lethal chemicals were injected into the veins of her other patients, her library set on fire. Seasons simultaneous: fall's spring and winter's summer chased in fragments down the hall or – captured and cut to pieces – stuck burning to the ceiling.

As I explored the spa, I attempted to see the rooms as they

had been. Each room was a hieroglyph which I had to decipher. This became my way of reconstructing a past, a memory, a life.

The spa was my inscribed tomb. I plumbed its precious mystery, the dark surfaces of its midnight floors, the walls washed clean in the early-morning light. I strained my ears to hear the small toccatas of forks and pressed my face into the threadbare drapes angling, like Bottlenose, for dispersed perfumes.

I was my own archaeologist. I populated the empty opera house, a place as silent as sidereal space, with tootling, sequined women and their bowing-and-scraping mates. I imagined that adulterers agitated the bougainvillaea, that maidens hung suspended in the waters of the wells, and – as I stood alone in one such cratered room – I dreamed of women soaking naked, their hair tucked under turbans; I conjured their fresh voices, their laughter mingling with the sound of running water.

I evoked the conversations of aristocrats and artists, the eccentric demands of arthritic spinsters in the massage parlour, the intense humiliation (as K described it) of an aging widower whose jet-black hair turned green under the sun; the haggard profiles of diplomats gossiping in their pyjamas.

In a white room where the cobbler once hammered out his shoes, the air still smelled of leather. And I wondered to think that as I lay dreaming of baboons the world was ravaged twice by war.

One night I awoke to the sound of the cobbler's hammer and knew I had succeeded where all other mortals had failed, except, perhaps, the great necromancers of ancient days. . . .

Ghosts resist the senses. They sublimate walls, annul calendars and clocks; their scorn of time and matter is legendary. Within a month I had raised a figment with my mind, and, as I crept down the hall towards the cobbler's room, I savoured the sounds of a conjured hammer striking the volatile essence of a shoe.

When I stood in darkness before the open door it was as if the air had gelled. Radiating reflected moonlight it quivered. The cobbler, mad, muscular and stooped, materialized holding a hammer in one hand and in the other a green shoe. I knew, although I cannot say why, that the shoe was intended for Odille. I felt a weight lift from my heart when this vision, like a reach of sand undone by water, collapsed.

The next day I was not surprised to see the spoor of human footsteps in the dust of all the rooms. In a turquoise chamber painted with dolphins, I found a ghostly rose which fell to pieces in my hand. The faded petals had a fragrance I recognized; the rose came from K's west garden. And when I crushed the petals and held them to my lips, I heard, somewhere near the ceiling, the voice of a soprano K once described who – in an ebony bed sold at Drouot for a tenth its value – had entertained the spa's handsomest clients, male and female, and who had insisted upon fresh rose petals in her bed, her wine, her bath. That derelict voice struggled to a shrill complaint before dissolving.

Then came a half-century of sound – dead marches, lullabys, the thunder of boots and distant bombings, of bodies colliding into furniture, of waltzes wafting up from the ballroom, of kisses, of doors slamming in the wind, of feeble ballads of wheelchairs in need of oil; and glimpses of the lovers embracing beneath a mantle of dust in a room smelling of steaming towels and broccoli. Just as my exasperated senses had been stretched to the point of snapping, the noises stilled to silence and the smells were only those of my lunch – a *pot-au-feu* of beef and marrow bones and cabbage, heightened, as I had requested, with one cloved onion (in Rose's manner). I padded down the halls in my felted slippers and entered a room which, until then, had kept its secrets to itself and where

I found a small, very worn toy monkey, apparently abandoned for many years and dressed in a soiled blue jacket.

It is uncanny, K wrote to me later, *how animals intrude upon our lives, imparting a symbolic potency.* As I examined the doll, I could not help but think of those other apes who had so informed my life. Crouching there I felt that the very atmosphere curded with possibility, that eager spirits were conspiring to give nothing a palpable consistency. Again I heard a hammering and saw, just beyond the door, a vitrification of the air, a calcification of the vision – the cobbler so material he could have bled, his copper studs on fire in the dark, his hammer making sparks in the mealy air. When he looked at me, when his abrasive eyes met mine, I knew I was seeing Toujours-Là, that the cobbler and the ship's carpenter were one. I supposed such queer marriages common in Hell.

I stood and stared as the cobbler-carpenter disintegrated into granulets the size of poppy seeds, as the puissant weight of the present pulverized him and his hammer, as his eyes flaked into blackness, his studs melted down to stippled shadows on the floor. But when he crumbled into the last vestiges of sabulous stuff and the room was pervaded, particle by particle, with a brighter moonlight, I saw – squatting in the centre of the room and staring back at me – *a living child*. His skin was white as milk and his hair yellow as flame. He was barefoot and wearing nothing but a pair of short, threadbare trousers, and the room was permeated with the earthy smell of his naked skin. When he reached out his hand, I knew that the little toy ape I held was his.

I have been hallucinating, I wrote to K, *but shall no longer. As it turns out the spa is haunted by a very real little boy. I've only glimpsed him, but expect to see more of him. By the way, the night you left I had the strangest dream. Here it is as promised:*

I am sitting alone in a darkened theatre facing the stage. The curtains are black velvet and painted with silver moons. They open to reveal a gigantic female, painted head to foot in bronze paint and carrying a bronze porringer – like a banquet-sized soup tureen. She bows to me and opening her mouth wide, vomits a torrent of blood. The porringer overflows at once; still she vomits. The blood gushes from her mouth as from a fathomless geyser.

I hear two voices behind me. Someone asks: "What is this play called?"

Someone answers: "History."

CHAPTER
18

Today I received a telegram from K. It reads:

A STRANGE DREAM INDEED, NICOLAS. *HIS* STORY IS, EVIDENTLY, YOUR OWN.

It was brought to me with my tea, in bed. I have been ill all week. Fortunately the housekeeper prepares my supper and my lunch. I suppose I look odd in my outdated flannel bed-clothes (the spa has a wealth of such things), and wool scarf, despite the warm weather – for spring has come to the Loire Valley at last – although I am too miserable to care.

This evening my head has cleared so that I may read – one of my greatest pleasures. Not only do books nourish my dreams, they engender them. I return to *The Fountains of Neptune* and the chapter which discusses the "Virtuous Abyss," the gnostic text which K chose to illuminate my case. Inscribed on a thin blade of silver, it was uncovered in the sands of Syria in 1939, and published in French translation one decade later.

In her Preface, K explains that *as a practising psychoanalyst I am interested in mythical cosmologies because they suffuse the hidden landscapes of the mind with light.* She continues: *Curiosity – perhaps our most transcendent quality – is kindled by our need to discover our origins. Looking for the "One Root" we are inevitably confronted with the "Forked Root." That is to say: the dual nature of the world. We pay for this knowledge with anguish. The purpose of myth, therefore, is both to reveal and conceal. To tell what we have seen and to disguise it, to mask God's forked tongue.* From *The Virtuous Abyss*, K quotes:

> *Mistress of Archons, She*
> *delivers the world*
> *from the filthy waters and*
> *animates the mud.*
> *She is the colour*
> *of water, the*
> *immortal, the immense*
> *Humid Element.*
> *She is Incorruptible Light.*
> *Violent agitation*
> *Power, Chaos, and Plenitude.*
> *The One Perfect Letter.*
> *The Virtuous Abyss.*

One might say, writes K, referring to my own mother, *that the Virtuous Abyss is Odille, all our Odilles: Goddess, Mother, Temptress. Her essential quality is ambiguity.*

It is because the Sandman's story, the story of a child who has seen by his mother's fault his father's face swallowed by the sea, that we may begin to understand a cosmology in which truth – which is the only "incorruptible light" – can exist in an abyss and so render it "virtuous." The ancient text in turn informs the Sandman's story, and gives it particular resonance. As was celebrated the Virtuous Abyss, so it was sung of Odille:

> *She was our sea of trouble*
> *our water of life;*
> *all our dirty weather;*
> *everyman's wife.*

According to gnostic tradition, the archons asked Adam:
"Where have you come from?" The quest for knowledge is first and foremost the quest for self-knowledge.
When the Sandman fell into his own reflection, he was

attempting to answer the archons' question. As we have seen, for the Sandman, it is water that holds the answer. Each reflection is a triumvirate: Vouivre, Father, Self. The metaphor could not be better: the Virtuous Abyss is no other than the female aspect of Neptune. She who "animates the mud" is mother of us all.

Ill health is the perfect excuse for reverie. As I lie as vulnerable as a newborn babe my mind ignites. I dream about the blond boy seen in a sudden blaze of sunlight, the motes of the air orbiting his head like the scattered sequences of planetary rings.

I offered him the toy monkey. He seized it somewhat savagely. I asked him his name. His mouth opened as if to form the letter o, but either he was too shy to speak or surprise had deafened me. His name remains a mystery.

As does the name of God, K writes. Perhaps the boy is dumb? Why wasn't he in school?

And if Paradis claims two lunatics?

I do hope, K writes, for your sake, that he will turn out to be both voluble and sane.

I fantasize that, having learned of my illness, the boy appears in my room with little gifts: a pressed moth, a cuckoo's egg, an orange. To thank him I tell him stories, the stories Totor, Toujours-Là, and the Marquis told me. And my own stories – don't I have fifty years of dreams to tell? I pretend he is standing in the hall just outside my door listening. Sometimes I swear I can hear his soft breathing in the late afternoon stillness. Yes! *He is here.* My nostrils flare with the fresh leaf-smell of his skin. . . .

Tonight the evening sky is spectacular. I leave my room to sit beside a fountain in a garden, which fades before my eyes, and I see the boats of the stars pierced by arrows of fire. A mist informs the air like a text written in an ink of sulphur; a calciferous haze clings to the skin of the world. The play of fountains feeds it and the terraced pools of naturally steaming water. One day the spa, steeped in its own juices, will lithify. Its pillars will rise like fossil trees in a lunar air.

Looking toward the topiaries I think I see the shadowy form of Figuebique. I blink, and then, looking again, it is gone. Unsettled, I return to the kitchen to paint paper flags.

Later, padding down the halls in my slippers, I enter into a sudden climate of exhilaration. Irrational as it may seem, I feel that a discovery of magnitude is about to present itself. Familiarity cannot domesticate these rooms for they will always be mysterious – after all, these are the bare skeletons of rooms. (And it is mine to clothe them with flesh and to wire the skulls for speech!)

The turquoise room, that chamber of special significance – for it is here that I first saw the boy – draws me to itself. As I walk to it I sense that it is waiting for me. When I push the door open it sighs. In the dim light of a rising moon, traced upon the floor in coloured chalk, a landscape is revealed.

It is a peninsula and it covers two-thirds of the floor. It comprises yellow beaches, splintered promontories, an expanse of desert starred with seas of salt, a tropical forest with elephant paths, and at the tip, a city, its maze of streets and towers protected by an outer wall, an inner wall, and a moat. Mountains as cusped as the jaws of crocodiles rise where the peninsula touches the wall.

Falling to my knees I squint at the floor. Along the shoreline I see words. They have been badly smeared, but upon reflection I am able to decipher:

the Kingdom of d'Elir

Now I spend all my waking hours collecting signs, fragments of the boy's passing and clues to his games or, rather, the One Game, as it appears to be. I find the next clue on the ballroom floor – a diagram drawn in coloured chalk one metre high – and, because it has been almost entirely wiped away, almost impossible to decipher. It appears to have been a laddered graph, or species of family tree, consisting of rectangles of various sizes and a curious network of black arrows. The whole had been drawn with great care only to be hastily erased. Perhaps the boy was made suddenly aware of my proximity as I, in my morbid need to wander, shuffled from room to room? Standing over it I get the feeling of being on the edge of something unattainable, a valley of diamonds that can be reached only by eagles.

Late this afternoon, I write to K, *I looked in on the turquoise room. Something important is happening to me. I see the chalked peninsula with clarity; its sight quickens me. I am enchanted by the child and his play. I long to uncover the mystery of the barely discernible, yet carefully traced ladder of laws or mythological chart – whatever it may be.*

CHAPTER

19

Sometimes I walk with my face to the ground contemplating the sand in the path, and sometimes I see small fossils – tiny sea urchins, sand dollars the size of tacks, the obsidian gleam of a shark's tooth. Or I look to the sky. At night I contemplate the moon. It always takes me back to Toujours-Là; it always takes me back to Odille.

Once when the moon's full face illuminated the paths of sand I entertained this reverie: I imagined a planet where languages grow as spontaneously as crystals; I pretended that the fossils – so perfectly round – were the seeds of new moons.

Today at noon the Heavens are exceptional. Both spheres are visible and the arc of the sky shines hard and bright like polished metal. I suppose I look foolish ambling along with my eyes glued to the sky, now to the ground; I suppose I look like something a brilliant boy might point a finger at. I know how odd I am, skinny and stooped, bleary-eyed, with a red beak. But as I walk along, my attention is captured by a thickening line traced deeply in the sand. Within the garden path a smaller path appears. It leads to the poplar grove.

At the centre of a circle of trees, bright in the noonday sun, stands a small pyramid of sand. And at the summit, sitting on a smooth, white stone (I recognize a marble flagstone from the spa's east terrace) sits the toy ape dressed in a cape of silver paper. Scratched into the sand at the foot of the pyramid are these words:

The throne of the DECaGon
ORDER & system are necessary in everything.

In the stillness of the afternoon I stand in deep contempla-
tion of the monkey on the mound. With nostalgia I recall my
childhood companion: Thingummy Ma'Hoot – that delphic
crockery which, secreted beneath my pillow, gave direction
to my thoughts. I remember how, beneath Thingummy's gaze,
I caressed Odille's belly with one thumb and with the other,
Erzulie. I did this so long and so often that soon my mother's
belly was as worn away as her face.

I stand thus for what must be a very long time. When the
sound of footsteps tears at the skin of my dream, the sun is low
on the horizon. I turn just in time to see the boy running
through the trees towards the road to Paradis. He is so close I
can hear chalk dancing like bones in his pocket.

"Wait!" I cry. "Please wait!" He ignores me. It is likely he
has heard strange things about me. My barking, for instance,
my hermit ways, my more than peculiar history. Surely he
wants to play, and yet he doesn't dare. As he runs, I feel my
thick dreamer's blood hasten. Down, through the cypress valley, down the distant, wooded road, which tugs and bends
beyond the northwest willows all in leaf, golden in the evening, I follow him. He tugs at my heart, this boy. Would that I
were what he is. Would that I were he! Running towards
some childish adventure, captivated by the game. Whatever
the rules are, no matter how bizarre, I am prepared to play. If
he is "Decagon of the Highest Magnitude" (that, too, I saw
scrawled in chalk somewhere), I'll gladly accept a lower station, a "lesser magnitude." The boy! I have lost him.

For the first time I find myself alone in the village. I walk past the houses, their curtains drawn against the street, and smell leek soup and the heavenly odour of fruit stewing with cinnamon. The streets are nearly empty but for a girl skipping home with a stick of bread, a man ringing past on a bicycle. Despite the hour, I see that the *bazar* is not closed; the front door painted green, and, repaired with a piece of linoleum, it is held open with a gutted chair. After these weeks alone in the spa's barren stillness I am tempted to take a look inside. The proprietress is not a cordial woman. Thick, beetle-browed, asthmatic, she sits preying upon her knitting. She is partially concealed by a mesh bag of sponges, which hangs suspended from the ceiling.

I wander past mite jet buttons, survivors of another era, spools of thread laid out in boxes like collections of brilliant scarabs, small, black paper packages of gold-eyed needles. I finger these and realize with a thrill that their manufacture has not changed since Rose's time. The *bazar*, sprangled and shining, could have been chloroformed fifty years ago and kept ever since under glass. Watercolour boxes and glue like syrup in rubber-tipped bottles. Boxes of flyweight stars. Games of "families," and sticky-backed images of animals. I crave the *bazar*'s entire inventory. Wire crayfish traps. Boxes of copper screws. Baby dolls the size of thumbs and – hanging in clusters like grapes in cellophane – gnome gorillas with scarlet lips, very white teeth, and movable arms and legs. For an instant a beam of light slides in the door and sets the apes on fire.

I steal a look at the *bazar*'s proprietress. She appears to have forgotten all about me. I take a gorilla down from its hook and examine it attentively.

It is a cheap, plastic toy, but nicely made, the fur well moulded, the expression interesting. It looks intelligent – engaging and formidable all at once. I scrutinize another. Painted in haste, his eyes are ever so slightly crossed. Another

shares a marked kinship to Charlie Dee. I want them all. K, I
wonder to myself, is it foolish, is it folly, for a grown man to
want to play with toys? I imagine K's answer: But, Nicolas!
You've had no time to play. Enjoy yourself: If God exists, He
is a child at play.

"Thong Hong." The hag startles me.

"King Kong?"

"*Hong* Thong."

"My son!" I foolishly exclaim. Surely she knows who I am,
and everyone knows I have no family. But she shows no surprise and it occurs to me that my life is of no interest to her.
Yet I blush furiously and am shaken by a small fit of barely
contained barking. What compels me to justify myself?

"Tholdiers?" With a thick knitting-needle she points to a
sooty box.

"No," I say with authority. "I'll take the apes."

"*All* thapes?" Her eyes shine, not with curiosity but greed.
When she smiles I realize that she has a cleft palate. I think:
What an ass I am! She just wants to make a sale. I nod.
Clucking her contentment, she clears the counter for my pur-
chases.

I need other things. Scissors. Glue. Coloured paper. To the
sound of her heavy breathing I root around the place. Soon I
forget her entirely. Merchandise rises to either side of me like
the banks of Bottlenose's enchanted river. In ecstasy I steam
down the aisles. String. Those spools of thread. Thimbles.
"Order and system are necessary in everything." I reach for a
feather duster.

Upon returning home I light a gas burner in the kitchen and
holding the apes one by one high above the flames with the
help of a long-handled meat-fork, heat them gently until they
are malleable. I transform them so that each should have a
distinct personality. I flatten foreheads, cheeks, distend legs. It
is a tricky business and a leg is atrophied in the process. I

scorch my fingers. I do this with the windows open because the heated plastic gives off a dreadful stench.

The *bazar* had provided small spray cans of bicycle paint. Taking pains, I spray each ape with a veil of colour. I give one a bluish tint, a magenta belly to another. Inspiration dictates that an "Ape of Magnitude" should be white, blackened by the moon with sombre spots. I paint his buttocks gold so that when he bends over, lesser apes will be dazzled. I give him a thimble helmet crowned with the duster's finest feather. I make boots with thread of many colours, and silver-foil belts, and capes of stars. I give some apes wings; they look like the archons of a gnostic manuscript; I give each ape a gilded split-pea amulet to hold.

I work late into the night. More than once a small face peers in at the window. Before retiring I stand the apes in careful rows in the turquoise room. Back in bed after a bath I continue to read K's book: *By returning to the water, Nicolas simultaneously returned to the Mother and unveiled her. He returned to the Father and became him. And he became Thomas: his father's assassin.*

I fall asleep wondering what she means.

CHAPTER
20

She means that my drowning was an attempted suicide. But I insist it was an accident. When I bent over the water to look after Aristide's bird I leaned too far.

Once K asked me: "When you looked into the water, what did you see?" This conversation took place a little over a month after my awakening. We were sitting in the garden, I on my wheels and K in a wicker garden chair so large it made her look like a child sitting on a throne.

"I saw. . . . Once I saw my mother's face above me in a dream. It was white, white as the moon, in fact it *was* the moon, shining in at the window. It woke me up. In the dream my mother was wearing diamonds at her throat and the cleft of her bosom was dark, a deep crevice, an abyss – I was afraid of falling. I remember another necklace, a string of pearls. I pulled at it and it came away from her neck. Pearls spilled all over my face, the bed, the floor. Even now I can hear the sound the pearls made as they hit the floor and rolled in all directions. I can hear her laughter, the sound of my mother's laughter."

"Describe this laughter."

"Bells. It. . . ." And I was sobbing and could not stop. My heart was broken by the weight of my sorrow.

My little apes have remained undisturbed for a week. The housekeeper complains that they impede her passage through the house. I have fought with her. I came upon her just as she was about to mop down the ballroom floor. She insisted that she was only following Doctor Kaiserstiege's directions. And, as she also complained about the mess in the kitchen, I told her to simply leave a basket with my lunch just outside the door; to do this and nothing else. No longer ill, spry on my feet, I have no more need of her. I certainly don't want her nosing about.

In the turquoise room the Kingdom of d'Elir also remains untouched but for fine particles of dust accumulating on the city streets, the jungle paths, and sandy beaches, and even that maw of mountains on the wall. Dust adheres to those seven crests and muscled flanks like a snow. I like to imagine that the mountains conceal the warrens of dragons who, as they growl together, utter vowels of fire.

I sit for hours and watch the particles of dust falling – from where? And rising. This stealthful activity, as sunlight and moonlight reveal it, appears to be continuous. Sometimes more dust appears to rise in the air than to descend. Yet everything finishes by falling. As I understand it, this is universal law. Even Thomas fell beneath the weight of bodies and of stones. Vain and potent he was brought down.

Odille. My father. Thomas. As the story goes, within the hour all three – wife, cuckold, assassin – were dead. And I, the startled babe shocked into silence, wide-eyed and stained with excrement, lay looking up at the blessedly empty expanse of Rose's ceiling, that smooth pearl. I lay like a turtle on my back in that white room of forgetfulness which smelled of scalded milk.

What do you think? I write to K. *Our fate is Charlie Dee's. Sooner or later we all hit the wall.*

Ah, Fröschlein, she answers, *you sound so unhappy. But you see, the wall is only in your own mind. Live your life creatively and the wall vanishes, and death, when it comes, may be peaceful.*

However, it is too soon for you to be thinking of death. Think instead of all the untried years before you, the game only just begun. The Tex-Mex dinners I'm going to fix upon my return.

But I *feel* the turquoise room come undone around me. The floor-boards are loose, the nails brittle, the paper lifts like a scab from the walls. I leave the spa for new nails and a hammer; I lope along and sometimes stoop to drag my fingers across the ground. I feel that this way I'll get there faster. I like to run at night. It makes me feel invisible – although more than once I believe I may have seen Figuebique staring at me through the leaves. I often have the unsettling feeling she is there.

When I return from the *bazar* with the nails – and they sparkle as does the hammer – I set to work at once. I nail down the floor-boards in the turquoise room paying special attention to the contours of the peninsula. I re-glue the wall-paper as best I can and stick on stars. Stars ascend the walls and transmigrate the ceiling like a charm.

I am certain the boy will like these. I paint the floor a dark blue-green. The plastic paint adheres to the old wood like a new skin, and looks so deep I leap onto the island scuffing the olive groves. They will have to be redone. The whole thing will have to be varnished, I think, as I stand on my toes. Yet Paradise reflected upon the sea could not be more wonderful than the boy's chalk drawing.

How long do I stand there poised like a ballet dancer upon a painted lake? I stand for hours in the deepening night imagining a bedchamber carved within the living trunk of an olive tree where a man can sleep and dream of love. And I wish the child would appear to take up the little blue apes, given as God gave figs to Adam, without any thought but to give his son delight.

Dearest K,

The apes are gone! All day I have had a sense of stealthful activity throughout the spa. I stick to my room as to a shell; I dare not show myself. Sometimes my heart beats so swiftly I must breathe deeply and regularly as you have shown me.

I am making small repairs inside the spa. I am well and I am delighted that you have been asked to stay on another month. As for myself, I still prefer to be here. The place needs to be maintained and there is so much to think about! Perhaps I'll join you next year when you go to Japan since, as you say, Kyoto has those famous gardens. But who could have dreamed that they are interested in the Sandman over there?

Your Nini

Dearest K,

As I hoped the apes have been incorporated into the game! They guard the walls of the city, the paths which lead into the jungle; some stand at the foot of the mountains. The boy's monkey, officious in his silver cape, has chosen to rule with my moon-spotted "Ape of Magnitude." Six others, all painted a pale green and wearing thimble helmets have entered upon an unknown adventure in the desert; they march into the badlands single file. However, the child continues to elude me.

Nini

The Gnostics, as K describes them in her book, imagined the process of creation as a sequence of magical events to which God acquiesced. These events were burglaries. The lesser demons who created the world animated it with stolen light. God nods and an island is born from the belly of the sea; God assents and a snake slides hissing from a tree.

One night in June, I dreamed of an island of pearls shining rosy in the sun and another island – a knot of living dragons tied together by their tails and roaring their anger. In the early hours of the day I awoke to see the boy, his pale hair illuminated by the first rays of the morning sun, standing at the foot of my bed. He was holding the toy monkey before him with his two hands and he moved it slowly from side to side. He was humming an oddly dissonant tune, and the effect was eerie. But the proximity of his limbs, his eyes like hooks of flame, touched my heart as nothing had before. It was as if my simple room had greened with odiferous trees and I was Sindbad staring into the eyes of adventure.

The boy reached out one hand as if to beckon or command me.

"You know . . . I had a monkey once. . . ." I began. He remained silent. "What is *his* name?"

"This is The Decagon," he replied, waving the toy like a flag in the air, "author of the one hundred and forty-five articles and rules. Do you want to play at war?" He wagged the monkey in my face. "I," he said a little pompously, "am Olivier the First."

"Do other boys play?"

"Boys!" Olivier the First scowled. "There is only I." Relieved, I said I would like nothing better than to play at war with him.

"Then you must kneel." I pulled myself from bed and kneeled on the floor. Olivier knocked me on the head three times with his monkey. "Rise! Sandman!" he shouted. And, running from the room, he cried: "Catch me!"

I dashed after him down the hall flooded with light. Olivier had a manner of moving which was strange, graceful but strange, and he darted in and out of each room we passed. I lost him continuously but only for an instant at a time. Disoriented at first, I scampered after him, plunging into a room just after he abandoned it. In this way we went leaping down the halls, he with the toy monkey held high above his head and I barefooted, my nightshirt flapping behind me, the spa resounding with our laughter. I felt exhilarated during that mad chase, and clean – as if Odille and Thomas and my father had never existed, and all the old stories had been written on water.

Olivier ran into the turquoise room and stayed. I followed; the room was silent, but for the sound of our breathing, the blood thudding at my temples. Olivier stood beside the peninsula with the ape between his feet, his hands held to his hips.

"We shall be kings," he said. Taking a small piece of chalk from his pocket he crouched down and began to draw a map of the spa on the floor.

"This is my kingdom," he said, hastily sketching the second storey, "and this" – he marked the attic with a large cross – "is where the wars began. You came down from the mountains – it was treacherous of you to do that; we'd signed a treaty, and these" – he pointed to three rooms in the south wing – "are the imperial stables."

"Horses!" I approved. "But I'd never break a treaty."

"Motorcars," he corrected. "You did! The war's been on for ages." He pointed out copper mines, treasure stores, an elephant graveyard. "Fossil ivory," he said.

"Tusks!" I said. "And skulls." He nodded. "My Assembly uses the skulls for seats. Officers sit according to their magnitudes. Pentagons, tetragons sit on the floor. Our warriors sit on heaps of dried dung.".

A crash came from the kitchen – the sound of a large kettle falling, followed by a loud curse. The housekeeper had returned for the morning. Leaping to his feet, Olivier ran from the room and into the hall. I ran after him. "Stay!" I cried. But then the housekeeper was shouting from the bottom of the stairwell; I looked down and saw her pink housedress swelling beneath me like a poisonous plant. She was looking concerned and even angry, although I am no concern of hers and in no way deserve her anger. She was asking my preference for lunch, was preparing a stew: noodles or dumpling?

"Hang the dumpling!" I shouted down, furious. "Hang the noodles! And hang yourself as well!" I dashed off, eager to catch up with Olivier. But he was gone, and the game, for that day at least, disrupted beyond repair. I ran after the housekeeper instead and attempted to excuse myself.

Tearfully she accepted my apology and blew her nose into her apron. The persistence with which she continued to be preoccupied with the problem of lunch recalled Rose. Flooded with shame I allowed that it would not be unreasonable for her to scrub the kitchen floor. I realized then that the staff she carried was a new mop. I walked her back to the kitchen attempting further civilities. I even went so far as to propose she remain all afternoon to scour the pots and pans, whatever; she expressed her pleasure. She said that I had frightened her – to see me running in the halls had convinced her I had taken leave of my senses.

"There was a child," I told her, "who I was entertaining. He's like a son to me – you see, I have no family." I thought: Here I am justifying myself again to these creatures. Why? But I could not stop myself. "Perhaps you've seen him?" She shook her head sadly and prodded the floor with the toe of her shoe. She sniffed:

"Perchance the patient was playing with himself!"

"Perchance the housekeeper likes to stick her nose in other people's business!" Decidedly, I had lost my head. "Doctor Kaiserstiege knows all about the boy," I fabulated. "He's part of her next book." I shuddered. What if it was true? "I have things to attend to," I continued, "and I believe you do as well!" Turning about with my nose in the air (and I believe at that moment I must have looked just like my old schoolmaster Shelled), I walked back to my room.

How I hated her (and myself!) all afternoon – because she was there like a boulder in the kitchen making dumplings and scouring the stove. How was I to concentrate on the game with all that mindless activity going on below? I feared that at any minute she would turn on the radio. Much as I wanted to, I could not enter the turquoise room. The woman's presence in the hotel made it impossible. The spa, vast as it is, had a way of shrinking whenever she was around. I stuffed my ears with paper attempting in that impoverished way to rid myself of her.

She called when the stew was done; her shouts tore through the paper in my head. I told her to leave it warming on the back of the stove. Once she had gone I crept back to the turquoise room. The peninsula fingered the floor in the paling light. Setting the apes aside I hammered copper tacks into the mazes of the streets, the elephant paths, the castle walls. I applied a second coat of varnish with a soft, camel's-hair brush. On the wet surfaces of the beaches I threw handfuls of white sand, the kind one buys for birdcages. The smell of burning brought the stew to mind. I pulled bits of meat and dumpling from the crust. Happily the hag had made apple-sauce.

Tell me more, K asks in a recent letter, *about d'Elir and its legendary geographies.* And I do, although she seems so very far away and the boy and the Kingdom so very close. . . .

This week in the garden we played at hide-and-seek. He has the eyes of an animal, they burn like two meteors in the dark. He came at me from nowhere and slapped me on the back. Dashing off, he claimed it was my turn to find him. I could barely find the path. We were in a cluster of hedges. I disturbed some sleeping birds. Hearing a sound I ran into the rose garden. The air was full of bats eating night butterflies. I stumbled on an ant-hill and fell. I lay on the ground and listened. The air was swarming with the cries of bats. I thought that if I waited he would grow tired and come for me. I fell asleep thinking this.

As Olivier explained it to me, a decagon represents an army of one hundred million. His ape represents him and his men. My ape with the gilded buttocks is an octagon and represents one million monkey men (of the race of Ma'Hoot).

We are creating armies of apes and those pink plastic babies transformed by fire and with glue. We invent all our own rules. We play with dice of our own invention. Each afternoon after the hag has left we sit in the silent kitchen, side by side, painting wood cubes with the symbols of variable disasters: demons, diseases and cyclones, quicksands and sins, treachery. Or symbols of good fortune: winter's passing into spring, fresh water and ripe coconuts (which multiply an army's ferocity by three and triples their speed).

There are startling, beautiful moments when Olivier will reach out across the table, and, grabbing my sleeve, show the painted cube gleaming like candy between his fingers. I admire storm-clouds, stampeding elephants, the hurling of lightning, migrations of fat geese. I admire a halberdier, a regiment, a musketeer: a toss and entire companies are lost. Mercenaries and their risks are defined by other tosses. Certain confrontations are decided by a play of dominoes. As are eclipses of the sun and moon.

Olivier names a hexagon Gilgamesh; I name mine Maximinole. For a time our favourite game is "Babylon." We float slave galleys in all the baths.

We have an entire room of ziggurats set down in real sand, a room of rivers, a tropical room, a room which is an island of ice. We have a moon game, an intergalactic war fought by angels and archons. We fight battles on rafts. We fight for silk, for gems, for oceans. We fight for salt. We fight against one another's gods; we invent gods – sometimes terrible, sometimes ridiculous.

Once we play at something we call "The Fly-Paper Wars" to disastrous effect. When the *bazar* produces a box of rubber alligators, we invent rules for this unusual army which has the firing power of archers, but which cannot cross the desert. We use tiddly-winks to plot our moves on the moon.

We build navies. *All* our ships sail to Alexandria. The second-storey hallway is our ocean. A coral reef of papier mâché stretches from the extreme north of the universe to the extreme south. This is Mondstato. It contains a monastery and a bird sanctuary, which the pink babies threaten to sink. It is guarded by whales, giant clams, and meteor showers.

Undersea activity threatens to destroy this lovely world. The monastic library, its portraits of magicians and kings must be moved. Olivier the First and I agree upon a temporary peace. We sit down together to produce these precious books, some on parchment, some on papyrus, some inscribed in clay.

The library, laid out in a red room, is protected by a moat of liquid mercury and a molten key. Back on Mondstato the monks, visited by a venomous cloud (three consecutive rolls of double-sixes) die like flies. Frightened by the stench of death the birds all fly away. When the pink babies reach the coral world on flying carpets it is a silent, deserted place. Even the whales have moved on to another room.

It would be tremendously interesting, writes K, *to see your library. I can't wait to get back home. Have you considered making up an encyclopaedia? You mentioned maps . . . a great carnival system . . . fire rites and funerary animals . . . sand paintings and insects . . . a princess born with silver feet. . . . I wonder: When Olivier laughs, what is the sound of his laughter?*

The sound of Olivier's laughter? It is the sound of pearls spilling to the floor, of bells muffled by a heavy fall of snow. . . . Is this what love is? I cannot sleep because he is not with me.

Nor can I think of anything but him. The Kingdom has become my world, but only when he is near. Without him it is a mockery, the shambles of a world: paint, dust, and shadow. It is his quickness I admire, his innocence, his grace, his fire. He is so mysterious! He is all I cannot know or name. He is the bone, the marrow of me. When he appears I am fearful, I am joyful. Olivier is that room I dreamed in a tree; he is love's animated temple and all the animals, new and playful, in God's garden. He is more than son to me, more than a friend; he is breath.

I have never asked him anything about himself. His past and origins are of little consequence to me. What do they matter? I think as we sit side by side cutting paper leaves and flowers that the entire kitchen could, by the power of his beauty, ignite. I love him because he has appeared from nowhere like a clean rain.

We are making trees: mango, coconut, breadfruit, banana, olive, and cyprus – those eternal trees. Ours is a universe in three storeys. Paradise is in the attic.

Is this what K means, I wonder. Am I "living creatively"?

You are living in beauty, she writes, *and now that the "rules" have been clearly retraced on the ballroom floor, would you please tell me what they are!*

CHAPTER

21

Dearest K,
One never tires of watching a child at play. I am mesmerized by
the nape of Olivier's neck, the way he holds the scissors, the way,
as he inks in the veins on a leaf or paints dolphins on the border of
a map, his eyes smoulder.

"When I was a little boy," I told him, "my uncle Totor and I
built a castle on the beach. As we worked, sand-fleas leapt about
us. These fleas are scavengers. They feast upon the corpses of the
same fish which, when alive, eat them. 'The ocean is one vast
banquet,' Totor liked to say, 'where sooner or later every guest
finds his name on the menu.'" This conversation put Olivier in
the mood to make a thumbnail library for the fleas and to give them
a world: Myopia. Sand-fleas are the only creatures in the Kingdom
of d'Elir to have developed a tide-pool architecture.

You have asked me why I have set myself the task of recon-
structing the world, or worlds – ideal, real, and imaginary. Just
after I awoke I had great difficulty remembering things from one
instant to the next. I could recall the past in detail – after all, my
"ontological age," as you say, was nine. But new thoughts,
perceptions, and even recognitions, were like gnats dancing in
moonbeams only to be snapped up, one by one, by a famished toad.
They would appear for an instant, buzzing, bright, and lively, and
recede into nothingness at once. My mind was a vaudeville show of
vanishing acts!

Ever since you left I have been going over all this in my head.

How you, with your affection and science, enabled me to regain entry into reality. I could have spent my entire life as immobile as a fossil in rock. But if I have been "present," I have also been passive. As I construct my temples and towers, I am building a bridge between the boy of nine and the man of sixty. I am reclaiming territory. I am making myself a country.

Nini

My Nini,
Your letter gives me such pleasure! I feared leaving you behind yet believed that you were ready, as you insisted, for autonomy.

There are many who would not approve of my methods and would say that you are still in the neurotic clutches of nostalgia and reverie. But I insist that the self is rooted in nostalgia and reverie, and that they are the fountains of Art. I argue that Art reveals the real. That the existential is always subjective. All that is true is hidden deep in the body of the world and cannot be taken by force. It must be dreamed and attended and received with awe and affection. But be careful. You are walking a tightrope. Madness is often the handmaiden of genius. To survive the world we must all be lucid dreamers!

Your loving Venus

Dearest K,
Olivier and I were sitting in the kitchen braiding crêpe paper into the bark of trees. We were speaking of islands. We both have a special weakness! I described Easter Island as I imagined it when I was a boy – with a Roc's egg rising in the centre like an astronomical dome. Olivier described an island gutted like a house and haunted by the blackest shadow of a bird; I believe he was describing a volcano.

"We shall catch crickets," I told him, "and bring them to the

attic. We shall open the windows to let in the sound of frogs, of summer downpours, and thunder. Unattended our Eden will spring to life.''

Suddenly I was visited by a stunning recollection of my mother: She was bathing in a metal tub and I was standing between her knees, supported by her hands. Her black hair tumbled about her shoulders like a knotted rope. Her nipples were erect and spurting milk. I seized a breast and raised it to my lips. With my other hand I toyed with her hair.

Recalling these instants my heart was suffused with warmth and I knew this was not a fantasy but a memory, and that Odille, as you have said, was not purposely evil.

Nini

Fröschlein,
I am so pleased you have had this loving, nurturing (and playful!) memory of Odille. More are sure to follow. After all, up until her death, you had spent twenty-seven months at her breast.

I think beauty is power. I think of the power and beauty of Odille. Had she been more loving than lusting, had she, simply, been plain, perhaps you might have lived your life like any other man. But no, it is not her beauty to be blamed, but her blindness. Self-centredness had blinded her. And famishment.

At a recent lecture of mine a student stood up to tell me that the gas chambers had never existed. His theory is that the Jews invented everything! (Ah! The torturous paths of paranoia!) I warned him that to ignore history is to sleep with a venomous serpent in the room. Those who think evil is but a lesser good take heed; it is above all a mutilation of the self, a plucking out of the eyes.

America is, as you know, at war. This war is televised and the abject horror of those images is creating a palpable malaise – that and the countless young men returning without limbs. There is a

new student here, a black amputee. When we met I thought of the
Marquis; I imagined him thus: a mime without a leg. The boy
introduced himself and I burst into tears. He said: "It's o.k.*, my*
mind is o.k. *I'm grateful to be alive." He said: "All my friends*
are dead. I want to talk to you. I want to know. . . . I want to
know why the human race continues to castrate its children."

Your affectionate Venus

p.s. *I've been thinking about Toujours-Là. It is evident he had a*
keen distrust of women. When I think back on everything you've
told me, all his stories were about ogresses but one – the one about
Bottlenose. As if that phallic-faced explorer (who even as an
infant tempted nuns) was the only hero who could fearlessly pene-
trate the female (this is how I read the jungle). But wait! How
does that story end? Bottlenose succumbs to fever beside the pho-
tographer's (!) skeleton. So you see, in the end all men (according
to Toujours-Là) fall into the Abyss! I cannot help but wonder:
What was his own story? Back to Odille. Had she been "virtu-
ous" Toujours-Là would not have loved her. He feared and loved
and hated her, just as he feared and loved and hated the sea. Yet had
Odille been virtuous, he would have surely damned her for a prig!

Your own Venus

Dearest K,
I am devouring your library. I have read that according to Ezekiel
there were no trees in Eden but precious stones instead; others say
those burning stones were stars and that Eden was never on Earth
but in Heaven. I imagine an Eden of trees constellated with
precious stones.

Enoch says Eden is an arid place dwarfed by mountains and
animated by columns of fire so high they obliterate the sky. A
desert, mountains, a pit of fire, and God's own hideous alabaster
throne.

The second time Enoch visits Eden he finds aromatic trees. The perfume of one of these is so wonderful it causes his heart to beat faster. Its fruit grows in full, tight clusters. Today I wanted to make such a tree but I had no glue. Paste is something I've learned to make, not glue. The bazar has it. I always take the largest size. It is white, suitable for wood, paper, and plastic. It is very adhesive and transparent when dry. It takes paint and withstands varnish. Why do I go on and on about glue? Because it holds my little universe together.

I waited for evening. I rarely see anyone then. As expected, the bazar was open and to my delight, boxes of toy hand grenades made of pressed cardboard and suitable (with minor alterations) for the fruits of Paradise lay stacked beside the door.

I haunted the counters eager to indulge myself in some cans of metallic paint. I carried these and the grenades to the proprietress. She took up my purchases one by one and squinting, deciphered their prices. She had done something odd to her hair. It looked scrambled and fried. As she taped my boxes together I contemplated the top of her head. Then she handed me my parcels, but before I could look away, she had taken her dress up by the hem and lifted it to her chin. I saw that the creature was entirely naked and, crushing my purchases to my heart, I fled, howling. When I leapt across the threshold I stumbled and fell. My boxes collapsed beneath me with a dismal crunching sound. To make matters worse, I fear the ancient hairlip was sobbing.

Sunday morning I awoke to find someone standing over my bed. When I opened my eyes I looked up into a pair of nostrils. The strangers scratched his nose and without saying a word shuffled off. I dressed and ran downstairs eager to obtain an explanation. A throng of people were milling about the front hall. I retreated to the third storey and found an entire family picnicking on the freshly varnished ocean. Boys had discovered the bathtub dahabiahs and sunk them all. Gum was stuck to the sides of the imperial stables and the blue-tiled balconies of d'Elir, its forums and circuses had been used for ashtrays. All the catwalks of Corpus Christi are crushed. There were people everywhere and I had trouble getting *rid of them. When the housekeeper appeared at noon, she put the blame on the proprietress of the* bazar *who, she says, has been "spreading stories." I can't describe the havoc.*

Certain illuminated decks of cards are missing, and all the dice; above all the precious world-state constitution, nearly completed, is gone. I've locked the Grand Hotel, but all evening the gardens were pullulating with strangers smoking cigars and riding bicycles.

On Tuesday a journalist managed to get in by lowering himself down a chimney. He called the Kingdom a "heteropia," the objectivization of the symbolic theatre of the mind. "Those little Chinese temples are awfully cute," he said. "I want you to meet Yves Prouteau. He's the curator of the Museum of Modern Art in Nantes." I screeched: "I HATE MUSEUMS!"

"Yes! Yes! I knew you'd feel that way!" He squeezed my shoulders with affection. And, ignoring my protests, walked up and down my sacred and symbolic avenues exclaiming: "You're mad! Que c'est génial!" totally oblivious to the ceremonial significance of the paths he was obliterating with his sneakers. He prodded Easter Island so violently with his foot that it became unglued. Then he got down on his hands and knees for a closer look at the cosmological references painted on the palace ceilings of Shāhbāzpur, the powdered faces of the whore-priestesses of Hooghly.

"May I keep one as a souvenir?" he asked, holding up an oval sarcophagus containing the embalmed body of the Princess Polyandrous and waving it in the air. He began to take pictures.

"I can't believe my eyes – why it's an anamorphose!" (Catching sight of shrubbery and lakes.) We had a fight over the camera, which ended when I was able to grab it away from him and hurl it downstairs. As he left he cried:

"You're a genius! Don't worry – I'll be back! You should charge admission!" (People were standing in line at the door.) "Like Le Facteur Cheval! Le Curé de Rotteboeuf! Pic Assiette!*" What sort of people are these? I cannot imagine anyone honest charging admission to their dreams.*

As soon as he was gone I set to work attempting to repair the damage. I sealed off the chimneys with chicken-wire. Things were quiet all evening, but the next day at noon the housekeeper introduced that dreadful Figuebique. Elephant parts littered the kitchen table and a heap of papier mâché coconuts were drying in the oven. Figuebique confronted me with numerous and extravagant rumours. She claimed that I am "the evil architect of places of worship small enough for demons and constructed of church publications with the holy words of the blessed Pope commingled with the heathenish vociferations of psychoanalytical journals, the daily rag, and other refuse!" (My exact recipe! Add glue, water, and stir!) That it is known I entertain children in ways scabrous and unclean (this rhetoric is hers); that I am not only a dangerous heretic, a lunatic imposing hurtful notoriety on the town, but, furthermore, a pederast!

"A pederast!" she badgered me, jabbing at my diaphragm with one extended finger. "A Paphian demonologist who has turned the spa into a heathen temple!"

"Yes! And I am Charles the Second, too!" I roared. "Grandson of Charles Daedalus the First and son of Thingummy Ma'Hoot!" To prove it I leapt about the room, drumming all the while upon my chest. Figuebique grabbed her purse and ran.

Now I am abandoned by the housekeeper. It is fortunate that we had put in a fresh supply of cans. I don't dare show myself in the village. But it really doesn't matter. I've more than enough to keep me busy: stacks of newsprint, glue, and paint; cardboard, sawdust, sand. I've the library and I've Olivier. As we sit together in the kitchen painting fig leaves on plastic babies and giving them wings (these are the inhabitants of Myopia); we invent new games.

"You shall play at being me when I was a little boy," I told Olivier this evening, "and I, I shall be Aristide Marquis." I proceeded to tell him the story about the archipelago of Waq al Waq where a large tree grows whose fruit resembles the heads of human beings. Each dawn when the heads awaken they open their eyes and mouths very wide and they cry: Waq! Waq! Subhan al-Khalaq! Praise be to the Creator!

Your own Nini

195

CHAPTER
22

In a recent letter K proposes a theory of d'Elir: she writes that its historic and geographic fragmentation implies a refusal of *place*. She suggests the Kingdom is a denial of homeland, the denial of home. And the denial of Time – *that absolute fatality*. But I wrote back to explain that d'Elir is the attempt to embrace the entire world. To be at home everywhere at once. Which is why its Amazon embraces the Sahara, its Nile empties into the Mississippi; its Catskills sleep at the foot of the Andes. If only I could find a way to make it rain without damaging the parquet.

It is, after all, only an accident that I was born where I was and when. And if, as Toujours-Là believed, mindlessness rules the world, at least my own small corner is actively conceived. I say this with humility; simply, I am content to putter and paste, wanting nothing more than to occupy time and place *in my fashion*.

This week and alone I created the bar in Thule Toujours-Là once described; its beams and rafters made of the ribs of whales. He said the stars were uncommonly bright and the constellations strange so I strung Christmas lights, white and blue, across the ceiling. I call this place the "Snark" (another favourite theme of K's), and I have painted this above the door, the S like a bristling sea serpent – red, spitting a violet smoke.

This room was once a pantry, cool and dim, its windows so

pummelled by rain and dirt as to be opaque, silver in the sun. I've painted a mural – a stark, polar landscape animated by the snarkish silhouettes of polar bears. There are gulls wheeling in the sky and standing in the broken, black sea on a hunk of ice, a lone explorer contemplating the beauty of the world although he and the world are doomed.

I have set an oil lamp on a little table of worn wood and brought in two evil-looking stools. I have filled a whisky bottle with tea for myself and for Olivier I've made a pitcher of lemonade.

Outside it is spring, full and deep; the enclosing hedges have turned a deep emerald green. But waiting for Olivier in obscurity I feel it could be winter. Here the world is cubby-holed and squat, the gravity of history contracted and compressed.

Olivier surges in breathless and smelling of flowers. Faerie in the guise of a child inspirits the room.

"Tell me a story," he cries as he slides onto the little stool I've set out for him. I pour him a glass of lemonade; he downs it thirstily. "Tell me a strange story, but true!"

"I'll tell you about Odysseus and the Sirens," I begin, "or Sindbad and the Well of Corpses."

"No!" Olivier shakes his head vigorously. "True! True!" he sings. "And strange!" He worries the words like candy with his teeth and tongue. "Tell me" – he kicks his feet excitedly – "tell me a story about Toujours-Là!"

"I'll tell you Toujours-Là's story," I say, "just as he told it to me, myself."

"That's good!" says Olivier. "That's the story I want to hear." He bends towards me expectantly.

"Today I am Toujours-Là," I tell him, "and you, *you are me.*"

"I'm Nini!" Olivier agrees. I take an authentic-looking swig from my bottle.

"This, son, is wh-whisky. D'you know why men drink whisky?"

"No, Toujours-Là. Why?"

"To forget. To forget the piece of bone they lost long ago in Eden – along with their peace of mind."

"That's good!" Olivier approves. "You sound just like him!"

"You bet I do, little bugger, but dammit – I forgot that I smoke a pipe." The problem has me stumped but only for an instant; Olivier's bubble pipe is handy in his pocket. "Phah! Tastes like soap! You want to poison me, son?"

I begin:

"I was conceived of a dark impulse, yes! Of two lumbering beasts. I grew up in squalor well inland – O far, far from the sea! In a hovel rotten with saltpetre. Even the stone floors was crusted with salt. I was the smallest of four an' two babies had died. My mother brooded an' raised rabbits; she fed them with the weeds she pulled from the roadside. We wore rags and rabbit skins she sewed into little vests; we smelled of dirt and badly tanned leather and mostly we ate beans. But once my father stole a lamb and slaughtered it. My mother roasted it before the fire; we kids burned our fingers on the skin an' got to taste it 'fore these men came after my papa with pitchforks and a gun. I never saw him again for three years.

"I was four when this happened, see, an' thish waz a cosmic event – for if there was only one shadow in the house 'stead of two, that shadow grew. She *expanded*, see, after he was gone. She was bloated on bile and all our little world; that dark and crumbling shithouse smelling of dead rabbits and mildew was a world reduced to a black, hard kernel of fear. We was always bruised about the face and buttocks; this was her doing. She taught me thish important thing –"

"What was that, Toujours-Là?"

"That the essence of the universe ish ignorance, a mindless will to will. I have a memory from that time. I would be nursing a torn ear on the stoop an' watching the dogs fight over a piece of tripe. They would tug and growl, each to an end and they'd circle, much as the planets do, round and round. I had this metaphysical fan-fancy –"

"What's a –"

"*Your trap*! It was *she* controlled the weather – especially the darkest kind: storms, thunder and lightning was female in my mind (still is!). . . . She was *big*. A big woman. . . . Her breathing rattled all night long in our little hole like wind in an empty coffin.

"Me an' my brothers – we was like piggies scuffling in a piggery; we fought over beans and a bone an' our bare feet was filthy, we had lice. We was vermin feeding vermin and childhood would have killed me but I was saved by a treasure I found."

"A treasure!"

"You wouldna' call it a treasure –"

"I bet I would!"

"Well, maybe, Nini. Maybe."

"Where did you find a treasure! What was it?"

"They is always plenty of dung beetles where there is sheep pastures 'cause the beetles love the dung. One day I seen a beetle go down a hole, so I got a knife and dug in after it. They was this tunnel and a neat little burrow at the end. Inside I found the queerest thing, the queerest thing but also the most beautiful thing I'd ever seen. 'Twas a burnished pear, small, fit into my hand. It looked like a top turned on a wheel like I'd seen the farmer's son play with – smooth, lovely no matter how you looked. I knew it belonged to the beetle, but it did not occur to me that the beetle had made it. I imagined that the beetle had stolen it from the farmer's son. It was so dry and hard and pretty – how could I know it was made of dung? That there was a wee larval beetle growing inside? Sleeping in its little nest? All this I learned years later when it was explained to me.

"That night I kept the pear close to my body. I slept on a heap of straw with my brothers; as I was the smallest I lay at their feet and I didn't sleep much 'cause they kicked in the night. But now I had my treasure and didn't care. I breathed easy and slept.

"Daytimes I kept it hidden deep inside the straw. At night in the fading firelight I'd dig after it with my fingers; I'd whisper to it. It was my little god-thing, see; I thought it protected me. I did not know they was a worm inside but I was sure they was a *power* in there. Poor, ignorant Toujours-Là! The most powerful thing in my life has been my own bewilderment!

"One day my father returned; he just appeared. All this time he'd been in prison. I did not know who he was but my heart sank when I saw him striding into the yard, the dogs all cowering and whimpering. I squatted in the straw, scared, touching the pear and watching him. We was all watching him, 'cept her. She was watching me. She saw I had something hidden and she came at me. She boxed my ears till I was forced to open up my hand and show her what I had. And she took it from me. She put it on the floor and crushed it with her foot.

"That night I ran away. The land was rough, arid, and rocky and though it was near summer the nights was cool. I was scared, Nini; they was plenty of owls wailing in the trees, and even wolves. But I kept running. I ran nights. Days I slept a little. I stole eggs from farms and slipped into gardens. I discovered that the world was very vast and – far from home – strangely peaceful. The buzzing I'd always heard in my head ceased. For the first time I was hearing things clear – insects, frogs, the cries of bats, and barking foxes, the sweet trilling of birds. It seemed I had left a malignancy behind me. Once I had owned a treasure; I believed I would find another."

"Did you!"

"Never!"

"And then?"

"And then one night I reached the sea. I stood at the edge of a cliff and, looking down, wondered at this magical thing, this enchantment which had, I was certain, been kept from me, purposely. I thought a piece of sky had fallen to the ground!

"Later I came to a village of fishermen. I stood on the shore, and with wonder and envy watched the men and the boys – some my age – setting out in their slickers with their nets. A big, barrel-chested man pointed at me and everyone roared with laughter at the frazzled hayseed I was. I was humiliated and angry, but I held my ground. I burrowed my feet in the sand and fought back my tears.

"The man knew me for a runaway, and he saw my need. He pulled a wheel of bread from the boat and waved it in the air. I approached.

"You recall – I was swarming with vermin; lice had hatched in my hair. The man who was soon to be my master nodded and without warning the others seized me. I was stripped and rubbed with slime from the sea and sand – especially about the genitals. For the first and last time in my life I fainted. Later I learned that in those regions all the sailors are baptized in this way; none escape it.

"I awoke in my new master's house on a poor attic cot which seemed to me princely. I had been bathed, disinfected, and I did not recognize my own smell nor the look of my skin, it was so pink! I tried the door and found it locked. There was no way of escaping but I could not have gone far anyway – I was so weak. My master's wife came then with food. She was strict but childless; in time I became her own. They never asked me about my origins and I was eager to forget. I remember how proud I was wearing my first pair of clogs and the blue cotton of the fisherman! It was she who taught me to read. The book was the Bible and I – having never heard a story in my life – loved it, especially the notion that the world had been constructed, and purposely. I came to question that; it seems the only sense is the sense we give it. We are thrust into a s-s-snarl, Nini! Of snakes! The world crushes us blindly without rhyme or reason and we – we is foolish enough to wonder why!

"I return, see, to what I knew as a small, filthy child: the essence of the universe is ignorance! If there ish a God sh-she's as my mother was – stumbling blindly through a dark room and thrashing out in anger, indifferent to suffering, the enemy of dreamsh, of boyhood dreamsh! Tell me N–Nicolath – wash ish more presch-precious then the dreamsh of childhood? STOP FIDGETING! LISTEN! I wants you to open up your ears so wide a comet could fly through your head without freezing your brain! I wants to hear the wind going in one ear and out the other! I wants you to empty your brain, Nini. I wants you to get a big hole ready in your head for what I've got to say next because it is *the only story*, hear; all the others are just a lot of hot air, farts on the wind! So s-stop jiggling. An' listen good, you little bastard!"

"I'm not a bastard!"

"Yesh! You ish! We ish *all* bastards! *All* the sons of men are bastards! Ever since Eve cuckolded Adam with the snake. They's no man left walking the world, Nicolath, jus' half-men. The snake went up Eve's crack, see, an' *stayed there*. You put in your pecker an' th' Devil will bite it clean off! Cry! Cry, little frigger! Cry all you wants! Won't change nothing."

The sound of sobbing brought me back to the darkened room. The Christmas lights hurt my eyes, and the small, burning window.

Olivier sat before me, weeping. A fine dust of many colours powdered his face and neck and arms. The infinite scales of his skin acted as minute prisms kindled by a thing which glowed at his throat, a golden knob of amber burning there which he fingered for comfort as he wept. Shivering with shame and fear I reached out for Erzulie; yet as I reached, Olivier receded, and, melting into shadow, vanished.

Like a little yellow apple falling forever in space, Erzulie remained behind, but only for an instant. Seizing her I seized the air.

CHAPTER

23

I cannot sleep; I can hear the constellations battling in the sky. I am deafened by the clashings of cups. Lupus and Leo tear out each other's throats; Heaven is smeared with vomit and blood. The crab battles the clock; Vulpecula the little fox greedily devours the fish. The cusps of the stars are locked to the tusks of the moon.

Tonight the sky is full of arrows and furnaces and swords; it is like a vast fishing net in which everything imaginable is caught up and thrashing: hunting dogs and microscopes and shields. I leave my bed to wander in the garden and, looking up into that seething ocean like an overturned kettle of filth, I see Thomas and Odille being dragged across the beach by their assassins, their bruised bodies glittering with sand.

High in Rose's arms I see it all. Unlike the others, Rose does not shout; she prays. She prays to the One God who sits upon an alabaster throne in an arid land, beside a pit of fire.

Staring up at the sky, I am able to reconstruct everything. The entire scene returns with stunning clarity. I run to K's study and begin to write, filling up page after page:

My hands were pried from my mother's neck and I was torn from her embrace. As I was carried to Rose who stood waiting on the beach, Odille's body was seized and in an instant vanished beneath the bodies of the others like a morsel of meat beneath a swarm of wasps. Hours later when Rose forced my clenched fingers apart to wash my hands, clumps of black hair fell to the floor.

My mother's hair was black and her body was white. I need not close my eyes to see her mouth, rosy and moist; her teeth like those pearls strung into the necklace I loved.

I want to reconstruct her body, to make a room which will be a tangible dream, her reflected memory. I want a room in which to sleep: white and black and quiet and perfumed. I want a sanctuary; I want to enter into the body of Odille. To sleep there as if suspended in water, my thoughts – water.

I imagine a room without place or history, as round and as empty as a wheel. By a careful use of paint and perspective, I intend to circle the square. In such a room I will be like an embryo which has not yet heard the world. I will lie within the room in absolute stillness. The world outside will be only a dim smudge on the transparent glass of my mind.

I have chosen a room facing north. The light it receives is cool and blue. Its paper peels off easily and falls to the floor with a dry rustle – the sound women's skirts made long ago – leaving bare the perfect plaster as cool and as smooth as the shell of an egg.

It takes three days to scrape the ceiling free of its old paint which falls in flakes. I enjoy the havoc on the floor – an accidental landscape. Perched on my ladder I look down on mountains, glaciers, seas or polar ice, fossil snow – the after-birth of a sanctuary.

Scraping ceilings is a painful business; one morning I awaken with a neck cramp and have to soak for hours in the "Kaiser Milkshake." But when the room is ready to be painted I am dizzy with exhilaration.

However, in order to proceed I must buy paint – shiny black enamel, and white. I have no choice but to return to the *bazar*. I set off at dusk having shaved, paper stuck to my chin and upper lip. (I've not yet mastered the art of the razor.)

The *bazar* is closed. I turn into an alley and rap at the

proprietress's door. When she sees me she blushes, which causes me to bark. I apologize as best I can:

"I need baba . . . bla! Black paint!" I notice then that she is not alone. Figuebique is there sitting by the fire in a monstrous chair.

"Bah! Ah! Madame." She acknowledges my mangled greeting with a sneer. In the shadows of the hairlip's darkling room I believe I see other figures looming. A small clatter of spoons like hail striking a pane of glass convinces me – and the presence of an imposing faience coffee pot. Its spout rises in the inky opacity like the neck of an angry goose.

I follow the harelip outside and watch as she pulls an antiquated key from her pocket. How embarrassing all this is, I think, hearing laughter, I should never have come.

"I am so sorry to have disturbed you. Had I known . . ." my voice dies. But the lights are on and the *bazar* sprawls before me in all its lavish extravagance. Attempting to conceal my excitement I reach for the coveted cans of paint.

"You are kind," I tell her, "very kind. If I hadn't needed this so badly I –" I am tormented by the thought of our last encounter. I bark once briefly; she blows her nose.

"Nuffin', eh?" Although I long to take another look up and down the counters, I don't dare.

"Nothing."

She pulls a wide sable hairbrush from a shelf. Reddish brown, wondrously soft, with a thick, brightly enamelled handle it is impossible to resist.

"I'll take two." Carefully she wraps the brushes in white paper, cutting and folding and taping with such dedication the effect is hypnotic. She has uncommonly beautiful hands. I cannot help myself. "And two bottles of turpentine."

She climbs her little ladder and grabs two bottles of transparent blue plastic.

"And masking tape. What's this?" She has placed a curiously soft cylinder before me.

"Ith 'eu."

"New?" She nods. "I see it's new." The thing is wrapped in cellophane. "But what is it?"

"Broo –" I turn it over. It is a special sort of brush. For painting walls and ceilings.

"Thank you. I'll take one. You are really very helpful. Every time I come I spend money like water!" I attempt a little joke. "But I've kept you from your friends!" Elated I return home cradling my parcels in my arms.

To paint the room takes me all week. After three coats of black paint the ceiling is as smooth as a skin of oil on the sea and appears to be deep. Looking up is like looking into a fathomless hole. My soul is drawn into it. I think this is the perfect room: empty, walls white, floors flayed down to a smoothness. Dizzy with fumes, I fall asleep on the floor beneath the ceiling's black eye.

Sometime in the night I am awakened by a tremendous clatter. I hear the sounds of voices, a confused babble very like the gobblings and honkings of turkeys and geese. I wonder: Has that mad journalist reappeared with reinforcements? Has he broken down the door? Does he intend to take the spa by surprise? But then I hear a voice shriller than the rest, blood-curdling in its single-minded intensity, and to my terror recognize, in that hawking cry: Figuebique.

"*Allons, Mesdames! Après moi!*" She coaxes her troops up the stairs; the spa reverberates with feet. My eyes inflamed with turpentine, I crouch in a corner of the black and white room with only a paintbrush for my defence, and wonder what is in store for me. I have felt Figuebique's incomprehension and dislike from the start, but I am not in the least prepared for all that follows.

"*Allons, mes enfants!*" Figuebique approaches, hallooing in the halls: "He's here somewhere . . . follow your noses! It's the rank odour of insanity!" The fumes of pesticide, ammonia, and black soap seep under the door, followed by a spill of sudsy water. Pressed to the wall, my head throbbing between my knees, I shrink into my shell and try not to breathe. Down the hall a body collapses into the Tower of Winds; like dominoes its columns tumble to the floor, scattering grazing camels. A troika splinters my door. I hear a hammering, a mind-splitting C-RACK! as an island is ripped from the body of the sea, a continent shorn of its mountains, the Ottoman Empire chucked down the stairs. Hags ascend the attic to swamp Shangri-La, to pulverize the battle royals and royal regattas of Rangoon. I weep as holes are punched into the blue skies of Myopia; as its circuses, black sand, ice-chess, and dice games are swept into buckets and emptied into the yard to be carted off in wheelbarrows – where? The dump? The river? Dogsleds and toboggans are smashed with hammers, and crypts, dance-halls, cyclone cellars – I smell SMOKE! They've made a bonfire. K! I cry, my heart transfixed by certitude, K! HISTORY REPEATS ITSELF!

"Good Lord in Heaven!" Figuebique has discovered the Vermillion Room, its plaster sphinx. "Another Devil-God!" she caws as she casts it from the landing. "COME OUT YOU ZOOLATROUS HYDROCEPHALIC!" She's just across the hall now, in Hook Head's Room of Chance, a kingdom ruled by numbers. "No!" My cries die in a gurgle of new suds; the room's awash, my socks, the seat of my pants sopping wet.

Shaking, I pull myself to my feet; my shattered door is kicked in, battered; the ladies have crowbars. With the sound of a horse being pummelled to death, the door is ripped from its frame. And suddenly Figuebique inhabits the room, immense, incandescent with anger, her lungs bellowing fire.

"He's HERE!" She's surges in, followed by the Virtues of Paradis, abdominous and bumpy; all are carrying pails but for Figuebique who brandishes a mop. I catch a glimpse of the proprietress of the *bazar* crying in a corner, soaked with tears, sweat, or soap – I cannot tell – but before I can go to her with the intention of comforting her, Figuebique strikes me across the skull. Reeling, I fear she intends to impale me on her mop, just as the Cyclops impaled Odysseus's men before putting them to the fire. But no – I am instead thrown down like a piece of fish and crushed beneath the beefy buttocks and thighs of two driving, vortical daughters of Eve; one straddles my chest and the other my knees. Satisfied to see me immobilized, Figuebique congratulates her troop before barrelling out:

"Forward, ladies! No, let's clean up this birdhouse!"

For the rest of that interminable night I can hear their shouts of triumph, the clatter of their pails, their mops, and brooms – as those vandals engulf, cast down, and raze my valleys of diamonds, my peninsulas of precious stones, my gardens of Paradise, my beloved Kingdom of d'Elir.

CHAPTER
24

Olivier and I abandoned the Grand Hotel for the gardens: the rose garden, the poplar grove, the circular path, and the south-side oak which overlooked the gazebo and where I liked to sit with Olivier in my arms telling stories.

Olivier had grown not only smaller, but somewhat translucent, so that I had come to think of him less as a boy and more as an elf. Often looking into his eyes I surrendered to vertigo for there were compelling atmospheres and capricious weather to be read in those changeful irises threaded with azure and with umber. They recalled that small slab of marble the description of which so angered Maximinole. I still see it – the grotto convoluted, umbrageous and slick with moisture, the sea reflecting a sky heavy with mist and wheeling with birds. I can hear the waves sucking at the land's edge; I can hear the parables, the fables of water, the elusive but lyrical weatherglass vocabularies of water.

In moments tending towards lucidity – and these were not many – I feared with an aching heart that I was dreaming Olivier, that he was only the purest essence of myself. But then he'd return with such seeming substance and renewed vigour that my wavering delusion would pick up just where it had begun to leave off.

The oak tree smelled of sap, the shit of insects and their corpses, and, because of the fountains and flowers nearby, of roses and sulphur. Perched like the noonday cipher in the broad, black hand of a steeple clock with Olivier on my knee, I could not help but think that if time had a smell it would be like this. For the first time in my life I sat out in the moonlight fearlessly and did not bathe, considering that I was washed each night by moonbeams. Stretched out in the deep grass or curled under rampant topiaries, it was the dew at the break of day which – falling from the leaves to my face – awakened me. I became well acquainted with several birds, certain spiders.

Figuebique could have plopped me in the nearest insane asylum had she wished, but the word was out that K was on her way back and so I was left alone. I suppose Figuebique hoped my accelerating dementia would justify her vandalous zeal; later I learned that the story had hit the press and indeed I have a vague recollection of hiding in a graveyard of shattered statuary as that ecstatic journalist roamed the gardens for hours calling my name.

K's letters accumulated, unopened, beneath the door slot. The housekeeper, not daring to forgo her duties entirely, and feeling pity perhaps, left bread at the foot of a bust of Hermes each day and a covered dish. But prone to freakish mental oscillations, I was governed by a theory of mastication, the curative and purging powers of rose petals and oak leaves, and fed her food to the animals – fox, badger, and hedgehog – which still proliferated (all this having taken place prior to the construction of the high-rises overlooking the river, the shopping mall and highway).

Haunting the gardens, then, stooped so that my fingers scraped the ground as I lumbered hither and thither, barking at butterflies and bees, I, the Sandman, had become something of an ape. When I sat in the tree scratching myself, or nested in a heap of last autumn's leaves, I justified my behaviour with thoughts such as these: The ape lives, just like the dreamer, in a state of moral suspension. Or: Running with the fingers dragging, the ape finds the nut.

Up there in the leaves it came to me that once war has destroyed all the cities of men we may well return to the gardens and woods to leave behind all the tiresome concerns, apparatus, and misfortunes of Homo sapiens, sapiens, faber erectus. Having learned to cherish transparency over and above opacity, I, gazing at the sky, did not miss my black ceiling. The mastication of leaves and petals occupied most of my time, and the spectacle of dragonflies in aerial copulation.

Mastication and meditation. A mouthful and a mindful. I thought: What more do I need? Long hours did I consider the lives of men and monkeys and told Olivier – now so diminutive as to sit in the palm of my hand – about the inevitably tragic confrontation.

"The night Toujours-Là killed Charlie Dee," I began, "Totor told me about a shipboard drama which took place in the 1880s. Small, red monkeys with golden manes and eyes of gold, and monkeys with thick, ringed tails, and noses the texture of licorice, and blond apes with long, sensitive fingers, and capable of smiling – were all kept in chains in the hold of a black and infamous ship aptly named the *Nosferatu*.

"The *Nosferatu* sailed from Sidney to Abijan, Le Havre and Amsterdam, and these creatures were intended for the zoos of Holland and Germany and Denmark and France. Somewhere in the middle of the sea they all sickened and died; their smoking corpses which smelled of charred forests and clotted blood were fed to sharks.

"One survived: a tiny, pink marmoset with white whiskers and a nervous tic. The captain kept her in his cabin where the beast's shrill complaints kept the crew awake; the captain was a cruel man. The marmoset, which the crew had baptized with whisky, grew wild with despair. She lost all her fur from pure anxiety and then, driven to a fury, tore off her tormentor's ear with her teeth. He had her hung from the mast-head but his wound was gangrenous and within hours he died of brain fever.

"And there's another story, far stranger. A Dutch spinster lived alone in Amsterdam in a small, neat house built of purple bricks. She had no friends but lived in solitude conversing only with the baker and greengrocer. Once when after a week had passed neither merchant had seen her, they set off together in the evening to her house. When repeated knocking went unanswered they fetched a policeman who, fearing foul play, broke down the door.

"In the kitchen they saw that the table had been set for two: two cups, two saucers, and two spoons. In the bedroom they found the spinster dressed like a bride in a white satin gown and stretched out dead. A little monkey lay dead beside her. He was dressed like a groom in a tiny pair of striped silk pyjamas. Both the monkey and his bride were wearing wedding rings and both had died of poison.

" 'You see,' Totor explained to me, 'their love was impossible, but it was pure, I think, and somehow admirable.'

" 'Pure!' Rose had bellowed, 'Pure! Their love was Peruvious, Victor! And all your stories Peruvious, too! You only tell them to taunt me. Poor, tainted dove!' She had crushed me to her breast. 'Poor conscience. Poor ill-gotten angel!'

"But the saddest story belongs to the Marquis. He had once sailed to Malaysia on a cargo where a Chinese merchant had invited captain and crew to a feast. At a table constructed especially for such a repast, each guest was served the exposed brain of a living monkey. Aristide looked from his bloody bowl of severed bone in horror and down into the face of the tortured creature, its jaw locked by the same infernal mechanism which held the head in place. The monkey was weeping and the fur of its little face soaked with tears."

I no longer know for how many days I had been sitting with Olivier on the black earth of the rose gardens pulling thorns from his feet and mine, all the while considering the infinitely possible shapes of biological, geological, and architectural structures – when I heard K's sweet voice calling me through the trees. Like the leaves her voice rose and fell with each breath of wind.

"Nicolas," she said when she found me, "please leave those bushes and come out. I'm home! And I've so much to tell you! I've some *real dollars*. We will get those leaks you've discovered in the attic fixed. I fear the entire roof needs to be seen to. . . ."

Although I was tremendously pleased and excited to see her, so excited that I began to bark, yet I held back and muttered (as she described it later) defensively:

"Olivier is here with me." As if his being there prohibited me from leaving the protective, thorny branches.

"Ah, Nicolas," she said, "there is no one here but you and I!" She considered for a moment before continuing: "Olivier is only a *figment*, dearest."

Looking down I saw that in truth Olivier was already little more than a scattered puzzle of fractured light bouncing from leaf to leaf, and flower to flower. Before my eyes he was disintegrating. Soon all that was left of him was an odour of clay heated by the sun and a waxy shiver in the air.

I stood up very slowly and walked towards Doctor Kaiser-stiege. As I approached her some subtle magic took hold, as if, by moving from the bushes to the path, I was no longer the helpless incarnation of an indecipherable secret, but a man shedding shadows with each step, setting forth on a voyage under the auspices of love. As if all K's letters, and our conversations in the past, and even my dreams of her, had transformed her into more than my doctor and friend, but something like a limpid mirror.

I took her arm. She had grown fragile; I noticed that she walked with hesitation as if she feared falling.

"How festive the old place seems!" she said. "A regular

fireworks display!" For the setting sun was striking the panes of all the windows and the Grand Hotel appeared to be burning. "A fitting setting for your Kingdom. When I arrived I saw you climbing down from a tree and so just dropped my bags at the entrance. I've not even peeped inside, *Fröschlein*; now you shall guide me! God knows I've looked forward to this!"

But I could only bark: "Doc! Doc! And sob and bark again.

All that summer and winter and deep into the following spring, K and I worked together to complete the revised edition of her book. A new edition was scheduled for the following winter, one in which I was to actively participate. Now the book includes my autobiography, from Rose's kitchen to the time of my drowning, the transcripts of my sleeper's babbling and those dreams I recall with clarity, the more pertinent aspects of the analysis, unorthodox as it was, and a detailed description of the Kingdom of d'Elir including maps and descriptive drawings.

The last week of August, Doctor Kaiserstiege wrote the final pages and the same week she had this dream: She saw three women, one young, one middle-aged, and one very old, holding a bright thread of glass which, as she looked on, began to vibrate wildly. K recognized the Fates and knew that the thread was her own heart. At breakfast – and we were in the garden – K said:

"Nicolas, I know I shall join the Marquis soon beside that deepest fountain of all, which is Death. Perhaps he will come to greet me. Perhaps he will be followed by the others: Totor, Rose, Toujours-Là, your father, Odille, and even Thomas. Then their faces (and their secrets) will be known to me at last, illuminated, I imagine, by Bottlenose's wonderful lantern."

That night, she read me the ending she had written for our book, its final page:

"*The Sandman created a dream-child which was his way of creating a self, and a dream-world because he was a stranger to this one. Like Troy all his cities were built upon ruins, and just as the historical evidence to his trauma had been deeply buried, so were d'Elir's foundations deep. Despite the zeal with which the village wives scoured and scrubbed (and as soap and water were not enough, they used chemical paint strippers and even brought in an electric sander), traces of subterranean vaults and vestigal walls remain etched in the surface of the parquet – very like the paths termites leave beneath the bark of fallen trees.*

"*I wish I had seen the Kingdom of d'Elir, its aquariums, tar pits, and gasworks; its porous cliffs and smugglers' paths, the short, square towers and marble thresholds of its ideal Egypt. I wish I had seen Mondstato, its dim monastic cells, and read its chronicles; seen the metaphorical reconstruction of Babylon and Venice and Crete; that third-floor ocean. Above all I wish I had seen Eden.*

"*By bringing together disparate times and places, the Sandman had dissolved History. To reconstruct his own story he began by building Eden – a metaphor of the world-self as it might have been, had it been ruled by love. Trauma violated his infancy's garden; I should add: his infancy's right to Paradise. The Kingdom of d'Elir and its garden satisfied a nostalgia for wholeness and the need for new beginnings. Like all myths it illuminated a greater reality. This Utopian vision of the world was also an unintentional metaphor of the universe as inexhaustible mystery and duplicity. Beneath that elaborate (Arc)hitectural and botanical delirium lay coiled (one of the Sandman's favourite words) his own Gothic memory: Odille, the "Virtuous Abyss" which informed his life. This d'Elirium was ruled by ambiguity.*

But as beautiful as d'Elir must have been, I imagine it was also a pathetic place because it was, after all, artificial: the universe reduced to sign, the world as book; an isolated object too small, too illusory for its own inventor to enter.

"Is this God's dilemma, I wonder, to have created a world he cannot participate in because it is too small for his aspirations? In the end the creators of d'Elir can only be confronted by the unattainable nature of all worlds – real and imagined; the intrinsically enigmatic character of everything: real, imagined, and dreamed."

The empty spa is mine alone in which to dwell in animated quietude. I have become a curator of silence, of fountains, and a grave.

Recently the eminent Doctors Tsukuri Nikki and Jiroku Nikki of Japan's Institute for Psychoanalytic Study came to pay their respects. Twin brothers, they each carried a white chrysanthemum. As they stood beside K's grave, Doctor Tsukuri Nikki said:

> "Our Mistress's boat
> ignites with flowers.
> The brightness lasts."

They expressed a desire to question me, "Venerable Sandman," but I declined explaining that everything they could possibly wish to know is already in the book. They apologized profusely, and, bowing in a charming way they had, took their leave of me.

What I said is not true; no book can contain an entire life, nor explore an entire brain. That exploration is my last, my only pleasure, and I indulge it all the time. My only other interests are tinkering with the motors of the fountains, raking the pebble paths (the Nikki brothers claimed they had seen no finer in the celebrated dry gardens of Kyoto and promised to send me photographs), and gardening.

If K were here I'd tell her: "I am a floater." And she would say: "A *floater*, *Fröschlein*, what on earth do you mean?"

I mean this: I am only interested in the allusive messages of my dreams, the innumerable spaces of my memories, and the perpetual wanderings of my thoughts.

One gazebo remains standing in the spa's south garden. I come here to reflect. Sometimes I indulge myself in thoughts of love. Oh, not for myself, but I imagine Venus Kaiserstiege as she must have been. When I think of her embracing Aristide Marquis there beneath the trees, I blush, not a little ashamed of my indiscretion. Yet it is a kind of worship, this reverie, and a longing for something I never had.

This evening as I sat watching the moon rise steadily up from the horizon I recalled an incident, long forgotten, which took place at the Snail and Shark. I had heard from Rose that the barkeep indulged in a "shamefaced passion for trash." This, Toujours-Là explained to me, referred to his interest in human biology. It was generally known that the barkeep begged from the hospital anything they would give: old uncared-for specimens in need of labels or alcohol.

One afternoon, when we had been left alone, Toujours-Là told me to take a look behind the bar. There in the gloom under the counter among the bottles of the more expensive liqueurs was kept a fetal monster about eight inches high. Its oddly massive head covered with soft, red down sprung directly from its shoulders; the little person had no neck. Mounted in its jar upon a glass cross, it grasped the horizontal bar with both its fists, and knees and body bent, appeared to be riding a wheelless bicycle.

It occurs to me now that, although the jar was undoubtedly smashed during the Second War, and the scraps of flesh reduced to dust at last, it still inhabits the keeping medium of my mind. That the Sandman is very like the floating monster, both of the world and not of the world, and – as long as I can hold fast the glass wand of reverie – somehow eternal.